Embracing Tomorrow

Tera Lyn Cortez

Original cover by Dark Wish Designs

DEDICATION

For you, with love.

ACKNOWLEDGMENTS

I am ever so grateful to everyone who helps my books see the light of day. My cover artist Rebecca (@ Dark Wish Designs) is amazing. My editor, Amanda (@ Dark Raven Edits) helps me catch those pesky errors. I have so many friends that I can brainstorm with and bounce ideas off of. (Miri, you are the best!) My ARC team is fantastic, and I have the best readers. To top it all off, I get the most wonderful support from my husband and my children. Thank you to everyone who pitches in along the way. I appreciate you so much more than you could ever know!

Prologue

The voice of the preacher registered as a hum in the backdrop, the metal folding chair seat digging into the backs of my thighs. My eyes fixated on the shiny silver urn, placed on a pedestal and surrounded with her favorite flowers.

That tiny container carried all that was physically left of my best friend. A couple handfuls of fine gray ash that would blow away in the slightest breeze if you removed the lid of the vase.

Toby lay quietly at my feet. Brandon sat beside me,

his left hand gripping my right. Tears ran unchecked down his face. My best friend had been his wife for a few short weeks before the brain tumor took her from us.

Friends and family filled the backyard to capacity as we gathered to say our "final" goodbyes. I didn't believe in "final" though. I would spend the rest of my life thinking of all the things she would miss, and saying my goodbyes over and over again as I attempted to come to terms with her loss.

I looked to my left, where Brandon's sister and her husband sat. Amanda, clearly pregnant with her twins. The baby girl would be Cassie's namesake, and I wept that she would never hold the tiny human that would bear her name.

Cassie's parents and two brothers sat directly to my right, just on the other side of Brandon, weeping openly.

The rows behind us were filled with people from the hospital where she had worked, and friends from all over town. Cassie had touched every person she met in some way, that was just her personality.

I didn't realize the prayers had ended until Brandon stood, tugging on my hand. I walked up to the pedestal with him, wrapping my arm around him for support and leaning my head against him as we stood silently before the crowd. Everyone had waited for her husband to make his final visit before standing.

We stood together for that moment, drawing strength from each other. Cassie had asked both of us to be there for the other before she passed, but so far we had done little more than float along on the same waves of grief, attempting to be one another's life raft in a sea where the pain threatened to drown us both.

The remainder of the afternoon consisted of more "How are you doing?" and "I'm so sorry," than I ever wanted to hear again in my life.

I stayed with Brandon until the very end, as we showed the last guest out the door. The two of us collapsed on the couch together, exhausted and full of sorrow. Brandon reached over and took my hand again.

"Thank you for being here."

I squeezed his hand back. "I'll never not be here. You're stuck with me for the rest of forever," I choked the words out through the tears.

Both of us drifted off to sleep on the sofa that night, each trying to imagine what life held for us without her, but neither of us really wanting to know at that point.

Chapter One

My phone pinged with the announcement of a text message. Grabbing it from the desktop, I opened it and stared down at the photo it contained. Tears welled up and my heart constricted. The text came from Brandon, and its contents had been highly anticipated for the last couple of days.

Two tiny faces looked up at me. One in a blue knit hat, the other in a tiny pink one with a bow. The twins were here.

I stared down at Cassie's namesake, the tears

flowing freely now. I wept for the niece she would never know. I closed the photo, burying my face in my hands. I sobbed for all the life that Cassie was missing, how unfair it was that her husband was sending these photos to me instead of Cassie herself.

Four months later I still waffled between abject sorrow and outright anger. Twenty-six was too young to die.

I had watched as Toby, her golden lab, lay on the back deck of her house, staring off into the distance in mourning. He had lain on her bed as she spent her last days in a hospital bed in her dining room, so he knew she was gone, but you could tell he still hoped to see her again.

I attempted to comfort her husband of only a few short weeks, as he wandered her house in solitude. Cassie had asked me to be there for him, but his pain was far more than I could ever mitigate.

Cassie's last wish had been to donate whatever organs were still healthy enough to be of use and then be cremated, so there was no grave to sit next to. Her ashes were in an urn Brandon kept in their bedroom, crafted from polished silver and much smaller than I would have ever anticipated. It's strange how much a life and body can be condensed into such a tiny container.

Toby, who was staying with me since Brandon hadn't known how long he would be at the hospital waiting for his sister to give birth, came up and nudged me with his cold nose. He whined.

"I know boy. I miss her too." I stroked his soft head.

I'd clung to Toby and Brandon like a life raft. They were all I had left of my best friend except photos and memories. Those of us who had been close to her were simply trying to keep our heads above water as waves of grief washed over us.

My phone beeped again, and the next text included a photo of the postcard that the hospital fills out for all the newborn babies. Cassandra Kate, five pounds and two ounces, nineteen inches long. Both babies were healthy and born at the beginning of the ninth month. It was followed by a selfie of Brandon holding his newborn niece, tears streaming down his face as he cuddled the namesake of his late wife.

I could feel his pain from all the way across town.

Brandon's sister Amanda had found out she was

expecting twins about the same time Cassie's brain tumor was diagnosed. Amanda had promised Cassie that if one of them happened to be a girl they would name it after her, and right before she died an ultrasound confirmed one boy and one girl. On her deathbed, Cassie learned she would have a namesake; a tiny little piece of her would remain in this world long after she was gone.

I texted him back. *She's so beautiful. I can't wait to meet her. Tell Amanda and Liam I said congratulations. Congratulations to you too, brand new uncle! :)*

I stated at the screen for a few more minutes, but no more communications came through. My mind wandered, wondering what Cassie's own little girl might have looked like, had she lived to have one. I imagined that similar thoughts must be going through Brandon's head as well.

A cool breeze snuck in through the cracked window, ruffling the pages on my calendar. Fall air had a significant smell to it, and it had definitely arrived.

Pushing the window closed, I stood.

"Wanna go for a walk, Toby?"

He looked at me and stood. W-A-L-K used to be

one of his favorite words, but since Cassie passed away he hasn't gotten excited about anything. Instead of his usual prancing and whining, then racing to his leash, he walked alongside me down the hall toward the door. It broke my heart to see how sad he was without her, just like the rest of us. Anyone who believed animals don't have feelings had never seen a dog missing their person.

Shrugging into a sweater I led us out the door and onto the sidewalk. My condo had a tiny backyard right outside the slider, but at twelve feet square it wasn't much room for him to run around, so we went on a walk at least twice a day while he stayed with me.

When Cassie first got her diagnosis she asked me to take him forever and I agreed. That conversation happened before Brandon proposed and convinced her to marry him. Since Brandon elected to stay in Cassie's house and sell his, we decided it would be best for Toby to spend most of his time in the only home he had ever known. I borrowed him regularly and always kept him when Brandon had to be out of the house for more than his regular workday.

We wandered around the block, taking a leisurely stroll. Aside from stopping for a few sniffs, the sad dog didn't seem to find anything worth his attention as we walked. I felt for the poor dear. He didn't wag his tail, and his ears didn't even perk up when we passed other critters. The cat that ran across his path didn't even make him twitch.

"I'm sorry buddy. Let's go home and have some dinner, alright?"

Re-entering the front door, I removed his leash and he looked up at me. His soulful brown eyes seemed to be begging me to bring her back to him.

"I wish I could Toby. I never would have let her go in the first place if there had been a way to make her stay with us. I would have given her my own brain if such a thing were possible."

His quiet woof was the only indication he heard me as he wandered away to lay on the couch.

Being single and living alone, I hadn't done much cooking before, and now I cooked even less. Most nights I made a sandwich or had a bowl of cereal. I stared into the cupboards, suddenly craving more than that, but the options were few.

As I grabbed the cereal box my phone went off.

I can come grab Toby now. Want me to bring some

dinner?

Brandon's text made me pause. Was he offering dinner because he felt obligated, or because he could use the company and didn't want to eat alone tonight? I had a hard time reading him.

Don't feel like you have to. But if you want to you can.

I tried to leave it open-ended so that he didn't get the impression that I wanted to avoid him, but that he knew it would be okay to say no also. I had been trying to cling to him less as time went on, knowing that he didn't need to feel responsible for mitigating my grief on top of his own.

We both need to eat. See you in thirty.

I shrugged, in spite of the fact that he couldn't see me, and returned the cereal to the cupboard.

True to his word, he arrived on my doorstep in less than half an hour, two white bags of take-out in his hands. Toby danced around him excitedly, stopping to peer around him out the door. It was as if he just had to reassure himself that Cassie wasn't following.

"Hey. Congratulations on becoming an uncle. How are you doing?" I laid my hand on his arm as I asked him the question, wanting him to look at me so I could get a better sense of how he really felt.

He looked down at my hand before looking back up at my eyes. "It was hard." His voice had a gravelly quality to it that it didn't normally have.

"I bet."

"An occasion that should be the most joyous moment of someone's life shouldn't have to be overshadowed by loss. They're beautiful babies, of course. Not that I'm biased." He tried to grin at me. "But she should have been there to hold them too." He choked up.

"I know..." I sighed. "As much as it doesn't help anything, I really believe she is looking down on us from heaven."

"I don't want her looking down on me. I want her here, by my side. God, this just sucks."

I took the food from his hands and headed toward the dining room. "Do you want to eat in here or on the couch?"

He looked at me. "You know, I think I am just going to go home and go to bed. I'm sorry, Jenna." He grabbed Toby's leash from the hook I had installed by the door just for it to hang on. "Come on Toby, let's go."

"Brandon I'm sorry." I turned, hoping to catch him before he left, but he made it out the door in a heartbeat and I wasn't going to chase him down, even if it made me annoyed that he didn't even let me say goodbye to the dog.

I could hear his truck rumble as he backed out of the driveway, and he seemed to be in more of a hurry than was really necessary. Grabbing my phone, I sent him a quick text.

I'm sorry Brandon. You can come back and get your dinner if you want it. I won't say anything else about it. You know I am always here if you need me.

I didn't want to say any more on the matter and refused to go hungry just because he left in a huff. Grabbing a fork, I proceeded to take my lonely dinner to the sofa, letting my mind wander as I did. The house seemed unbearably quiet and empty for the first few hours after Toby left, every single time.

It made me tempted to get a dog, but I knew that any other dog could probably not do for me what Toby did. He tied me to Cassie, allowing me to physically run my hands through the fur she had also touched, not that long ago.

Brandon had promised to allow me to come over when he was ready to go through her things so that I could get the things that had meaning for the two of us. Not that he would be ready any time soon. In the couple of times I had been back to the house since her passing nothing had changed once hospice came to pick up their equipment.

The dining room was barren and empty, aside from Toby's bed that had been put in there while we used it as Cassie's hospital room. The large window overlooking her beautiful back yard was kept shuttered, the blinds tightly closed. Her shoes still lay in the entryway where she had taken them off for the last time and I knew all of her clothes and personal items were still in the exact spot she had last set them. Even her purse lay on the island, the handle draping over the edge as if she would be picking it up any minute.

It broke my heart to see it all there.

But I knew he wasn't ready, and might not be for quite a while. Hell, I couldn't do it. We'd been friends for almost all of our lives and I barely had any memories that didn't include her. Without her, I felt adrift in the world. I could only imagine that he missed her ten times more than I, knowing he had hoped to spend the rest of his life with her by his side.

Realizing my dinner had gotten cold while my memories wandered, I gave up, closing the container and taking it to stuff in the fridge with a huff. Might as well get some sleep. I'd kind of lost my appetite anyway.

My dreams that night were filled with Cassie. The day we met in grade school. Taking driver's ed together and almost getting kicked out of the car for harassing the teacher. The trip to Vegas we took right after she found out how sick she was. Watching her walk down the aisle on her wedding day. Saying our last goodbye.

The scenes ran through my mind like one of those old fashioned strip movies that you could hear clicking as they played, even though the film itself had no sound. Eventually, they ended, and I spent the rest of the night in a fitful, if blank, sleep.

Chapter Two

In spite of my restless night, the following morning dawned as expected and brought me another sunny day. I lay against my pillow staring out the crack in the curtains, debating whether or not I needed to get out of bed. When Cassie got sick I had taken a short leave of absence from my job at the hospital where I worked as a billing specialist. I had tried to give them my notice, thanks to Cassie leaving me a chunk of money in her will, but my boss wasn't having it. He created a work from home position for me as a compromise, and I jumped on the opportunity.

As much as I loved it, the solitary days were starting to impact my psyche since I hadn't been making the effort to go out and socialize or see my friends. My love life was nonexistent, and I only had half custody of "my" dog.

I grabbed my phone, thinking a stroll through social media might encourage me to get out and do something. Instead, I saw a text from Brandon.

sorry

It had come in just after two in the morning. One tiny word. Five little letters. I couldn't be exactly sure what he was sorry about, and couldn't decide if I wanted to text him back or not.

Finally, I did because I knew that deep down I would do whatever I could to comfort him. I had lost my best friend and he had lost his wife. We needed each other whether we always acted like it or not.

It's okay. I get it.

Seven o'clock was early for someone who had obviously not gotten much sleep the night before, so I jumped a little when I heard the ding announcing that he had responded.

Wanna come over for breakfast?

I stared at the screen, biting my lip as I stared at the invitation. I wanted to say yes, jump out of bed and head over there. I wanted to accept this olive branch as a sign that we could move forward. But something held me back. I ended up compromising with myself.

Let me take a quick shower and then I will head over. Should I bring anything?

This would give me some time to get moving and not feel like I rushed out the door just to not be alone. I didn't want to use his grief as a band-aid for my own loneliness.

I got it already. See ya when I see ya.

As I dried off after getting out of the shower I heard my phone announce another text message. What he could he want now?

It turned out Brandon didn't want anything. Dana, one of the nurses Cassie had worked with at the hospital, had sent a message to invite me out the next evening, which happened to be Friday, to celebrate her birthday.

I liked Dana, a lot actually, but I didn't feel like going out in public. I sent her a message thanking her for the offer but declining. Stubborn as shit just so happened to be one of Dana's most prominent qualities, and she immediately argued, pointing out that I had turned down every single invite to get together since Cassie's funeral.

Guilt flooded me. I knew losing her had hurt so many people, not just me. And hadn't I just been lamenting the fact that my social life had petered out to nothing?

I agreed to consider it, and she told me she would resume harassing me about it the next morning. Her response actually made me laugh out loud, and it felt nice to find something funny. The laughs alone would be worth the effort of getting presentable and heading out into the great wide world. Okay, heading out to the bar ten minutes down the street, but whatever.

The drive over to Cassie's house, which I still couldn't think of as "Brandon's" yet, gave me time to ponder our situation. I couldn't be mad at him, not when I knew what he must be going through. It just frustrated me that I didn't know what to do to help him along. He had to heal his own heart and in spite of promising Cassie, I didn't have a whole lot of say in the matter.

As I pulled into the drive I could hear Toby going

nuts in the backyard, and Brandon hollering at him to leave it. Curious, I headed around the back to the gate instead of knocking on the front door.

"It's just me!" I called out as I opened the gate into the yard.

Toby came running over, distracted from whatever he had been bothering on the other side of the yard. Whining in excitement, he wiggled around me and licked my hand before running back to the shed and barking some more.

Brandon waved at me, then whistled and called Toby to the deck. Shutting the deck gate and leaving Toby behind he called to me.

"Want to see something neat?"

I nodded and headed his way. "Sure."

Leading me around the back of the shed he pointed up the large tree toward the hole in the trunk. Cassie had a pair of raccoons living there. After they helped themselves to some leftovers in her kitchen once – she had left the back door open all night and Toby slept in her room with the door closed – she named them Bert & Ernie.

I looked up, waiting for one of their little faces to

appear. In spite of being nocturnal critters, if they knew we were outside they always came looking for snacks. Bert appeared, moving out onto the nearest branch and looking down curiously.

Instead of Ernie's face next, a teeny tiny little raccoon nose appeared. It was followed by three more.

"Aw... babies!"

"Yeah, apparently Ernie is short for Ernestine or something. They're a few weeks old now and just starting to make appearances."

"They're so cute."

We stood together for a minute, watching them watching us. Toby whined unhappily from the deck, not pleased at being left out of the moment.

"Ready to eat?" Brandon turned his attention from the tiny creatures to me.

"Sure." I followed him as he turned and headed back to the house, looking back for one more glance at the little critters in the tree.

Cassie would have loved the thought of having them in her yard, and laughed at herself for giving them both boy names. We should have known that they tend to live in mated pairs. I sighed, wanting so badly to talk about her out loud, but not wanting to upset Brandon.

"She would have loved them." His voice was soft; barely above a whisper.

I reached out, gently touching his arm. "Yes. She would have."

He sighed. It sounded as if it came from the very depths of his soul. We climbed the steps to the deck, keeping the gate closed so Toby wouldn't harass the raccoon family any more at the moment. It was warm in spite of being early fall and Brandon had set breakfast out on the patio table.

We sat and served ourselves in silence. I waited for him to start since I could tell he had something on his mind.

"Why is this so hard?" he whispered. "I am barely making it through each day."

Toby whined and laid his head in Brandon's lap, trying to comfort him.

"I know. I'm so sorry. Loss is so damn hard, especially when it was someone as amazing as she was." I didn't know what words would make him feel better, so I tried my best.

"Before we started dating I'd been single for a long

time. I had no interest in settling down. Then she came into my life and had me wanting things I'd never given a second thought to before. And now she's gone. It's as if the universe gave me this tiny little blip on my insignificant timeline to be truly happy, just to yank it away from me again."

A tear rolled down his cheek. I reached out and grabbed his hand.

"I cannot even begin to imagine how you are feeling, because as much as I miss her I know I miss her differently. She made me promise to make sure that you didn't dwell on it too much, and I had to tell her I didn't know how. Her dying request to me was to be here for you, and I knew that even if I tried my best I might let her down. But I will do whatever I can. I..."

Of course, I started to cry too. He squeezed my hand, and we sat silently together, each lost in our own pain.

I let go of his hand and wiped my tears. His had dried on their own. He met my eyes.

"She asked me to take care of you, too. I told her I doubted I would even be able to take care of myself. And she laughed at me. Told me that between the two of us you and I could figure out anything."

I chuckled. "She's probably right. We will eventually figure things out. I remind myself that she would be so sad to know that she caused us pain. She wanted to be nothing more than beautiful memories that made us smile."

We finished our breakfast in relative silence. Once we'd eaten he took out his phone to show me the pictures of his new niece and nephew. Cassie's namesake and her twin brother, Connor.

My ovaries gave a shocking jolt at the sight of the two tiny humans, surprising me since I hadn't even been on a date in ages. Traitorous organs. Maybe I should get myself a cat or something.

I glanced up to see Brandon staring at me with a funny look on his face.

"What?"

He cocked his head. "You just snorted. That sound one makes when something highly improbable is suggested."

"Oh! Did I make that sound out loud?" I started cracking up. I couldn't help it. I'm not very good at keeping my thoughts to myself.

He just continued to stare.

"Okay. I had a moment of 'awe, I can't wait to have babies someday' insanity. Don't worry, it's passed and I will be fine."

After a second Brandon burst out laughing. A deep belly laugh that I hadn't heard from him in a long time.

"What?"

He shook his head. "I love that you label it as a moment of insanity and act like it was some sort of close call. A brush with death, if you will."

"Stop. It's not that bad. But seeing as how I don't even date, we know that the situation is irrelevant."

"But you will. Eventually. Right?" He paused, as if not really sure about me.

"Maybe. If Mr. Right comes along. Or even Mr. Maybe-he's-not-such-an-idiot."

"Maybe I need to set you up on some blind dates. I can round up a few guys and we can have a parade. I'll even vouch for most of them."

"Knock it off. Don't you dare."

"That's it. Cassie told me to take care of you. This is my way of doing it. And you can't argue because Cassie said. I have to do it. Or she'll come back and haunt us both-"

Both of us were laughing as I kept trying to shush him. "No."

"I can even have them fill out an application because that's what she would have wanted..."

"Stop! Brandon. No."

We both dissolved into hysterics, and Toby watched us warily from his place on the decking. I took a deep breath, attempting to gain control of myself.

He looked at me seriously. "She would want you to be happy you know."

"And I am. Mostly. There is no rush."

"Well, you aren't getting any younger..."

"You either old man!"

We laughed some more and then calmed. It felt good to have these moments, almost as if Cassie was around somewhere, just out of sight and we could enjoy each other's company.

"Thank you, Jenna. I haven't laughed in months, and I needed that."

"Thank you. I needed it too. And this is how she would want it to be. It probably breaks her heart to see us sad."

Chapter Three

The rest of the morning passed rather pleasantly. As I prepared to leave Brandon stood before me and enveloped me into a tight hug. Wrapping my arms around him, I squeezed him back.

"Thank you for coming over, even though I was kind of a jerk. I needed this more than I realized."

"No thanks necessary. I needed it too." My words were muffled against his embrace.

We parted and I turned to go, waving as I walked. Toby whined as I reached the gate and I patted him gently, promising I'd see him again soon.

The entire drive back to my condo passed in a daze as I pondered the thoughts of the morning. I'd never heard my biological clock ticking before today, and I tried to tell myself in no uncertain terms that I certainly wasn't going to start now.

But Cassie's death had pulled my own mortality into sharp focus. We were the same age; my birthday falling only two months before hers.

Common sense told me that I had a good many years left. Decades even. That I didn't need to be in a hurry to find a man and date and get married and have babies. Yet...

Seeing Amanda's twins had ignited something deep inside of me. A longing to hold a child of my own and know the feeling of carrying another life inside of me. Cassie's death had proven to me that if there was anything certain in this world, it was the uncertainty of human life. Nobody could guarantee you how long you would have with the ones you love.

She had been blessed in a way that she already had Brandon when she got her diagnosis, and he married her right off the bat. I'd be starting from square one. If dating had such a thing as a negative square, I'd be there. Dana called it when she said I hadn't been out since the funeral. This morning with Brandon far exceeded any other "socializing" I had done.

Pulling into my garage I decided to text Dana and let her know I'd be there. What's the worst that could happen? I'd be bored and come home? It wouldn't kill me. And I just might enjoy myself.

Dana responded with a dozen smiley face emojis and the details I'd need to join them. Sending a *LOL* back to her, I parked myself in my office to get enough work done that I wouldn't feel guilty about ignoring the computer for the next two days.

Usually, I didn't care if it was a weekday or weekend, I just worked when I needed to work. Today I made the promise to myself to return to some semblance of normalcy. I would work my forty hours during the week and take the weekends off. I would shower every day, get dressed and go out in public on a regular basis.

I realized how accurate my statement was to Brandon. Cassie would be heartbroken if she could see how hard I had taken her death, and how far I had let myself slide because of it. Her main concern towards the end had been that we move on. That we not dwell on her passing. I wanted to live my life in a way that would make her proud.

I worked for a few hours, then decided to pamper myself. I went out and got my hair cut; it had been far too long since I bothered with it. Then I swung by the nail parlor to see if they had appointments available. The universe worked in my favor and I got both a pedicure and a manicure.

On a roll, I swung by the mall and grabbed some new clothes. Jeans that made my ass look fantastic and a new pair of fall boots. As I walked back to the car with my bags in hand I smiled at the sunshine, remembering how Cassie and I had loved our shopping jaunts.

She had been a window shopper, content to browse miles of aisles and not buy anything if she didn't find that perfect item. I, on the other hand, bought all the things. If I saw it and liked it, boom! It was mine.

Throwing my bags into the back seat, I happened to look down at the ground when a glint caught my eye. Staring up at me was a bright, shiny penny. I'd have said it was new, but after picking it up I knew it had to be a gift from above. The year embossed read the exact year of Cassie's birth.

I took that moment to look up at the gorgeous sky and send my love for her out into the universe. I knew at that moment she must have been able to see me and approved of what I chose to do for myself.

Getting back to the house left me with three hours before I had to be out the door. The next item on my self-care checklist? A nap. Why not? Setting the alarm for ninety minutes later, I crawled into bed and relaxed with a sigh. Shopping had worn me out a little, and I had a long evening ahead. Might as well start it with a burst of energy.

By the time I woke up from my nap and showered, I had begun to feel that familiar reticence about going back out in public. As I contemplated texting an apology to Dana, the penny I had picked up on my earlier outing stared at me from the bathroom counter. If Abraham Lincoln could glare at me from a coin, he did it there.

"Fine, fine. I'm still going... I wasn't actually going to cancel on her," I muttered to the penny.

Then I looked at myself in the mirror. Talking to a coin. Lord help me. I really did need to get out more. I tucked it into the pocket of my jeans, claiming it as my talisman for the foreseeable future. Maybe it would bring me good luck in the dating arena. A birthday party was as good a place to meet a man as any.

Dana had offered to pick me up, but the idea of not having my own transportation to bring me home when I decided I'd been out late enough made me nervous. I had to have the escape route should I need it. About the time I pulled into the crowded parking lot it occurred to me I should have called an Uber. Oh well.

I found a place to park without as much trouble as I had originally expected and sat in the driver's seat for a moment. I took a deep breath. Why did I feel like I had a job interview coming up instead of a fun night with some friends? Checking my makeup in the mirror one last time, I unbuckled and stepped out of the car before I could change my mind. I grabbed Dana's gift, which I had picked up on my shopping excursion earlier, and crossed the gravel lot to the front door.

I winced as the loud music assaulted my ears upon entering the building. Thankful that smoking had been banned in all indoor establishments, I scanned the room looking for people I recognized. I heard Dana's laughter from somewhere over to my left and headed that direction. A smallish VIP section had been roped off to reserve the tables for the party and she sat in the very center.

I smiled as I caught her eye and she jumped up screeching.

"I am SO glad you're here! I didn't really expect you to come."

We hugged tightly.

"I said I would be here, didn't I?"

"Well, you're the first to arrive aside from my cousin who is playing pool with her man at the moment."

She led me back to the table gesturing at the chair next to her.

I handed her the present. "You didn't need to bring me anything, silly."

"But I did, so..."

I had picked out a bracelet that I saw in the jewelry store window. It had caught my eye as I passed by and it just screamed her name. Way better than the purse or scarf I had originally been planning to pick up for her.

"Oh my goodness, it's breathtaking!" She slipped it on and hugged me again. "I love it."

It lifted my spirits to see how much she liked it and made me feel a little guilty that I hadn't made a better effort to keep up on my relationships.

She took my hand. "How are you doing?"

I took a deep breath. I had mascara on and did not want to ruin my efforts by crying. "I'm doing okay. Trying to get better every day."

"And Brandon? Have you seen much of him? How is he?"

"Off and on. I went over and had breakfast with him this morning. Did Cassie ever tell you about her two raccoons?"

"Oh yes, the troublemakers. Bert and Ernie?"

"Well, apparently they are Bert and Ernestine because there are some babies living in the tree now. They make Toby crazy since he can't get to them, but they are adorable."

"Aw, how sweet. She would have loved that." Dana's tone trailed off as she finished her sentence. "I miss her so damn much."

"Me too, Dana, me too."

We sat in silence for a moment. Then I told her about my excursion earlier in the day and finding the penny on the ground.

"That was absolutely her looking down on you. I just know it."

I nodded in response, trying to swallow the lump in my throat and blink away the tears forming in the corners of my eyes. I managed, although barely, and stood.

"Let me buy you a birthday drink! What can I get you?"

Dana gave me her order and I made my way to the bar. The bartender looked me in the eye and smiled. "You look like you're in need of a pick-me-up. What can I get you?"

"A long island iced tea for the birthday girl over there," waving Dana's direction.

"And for you?"

"It's been a while. How about you surprise me with something sweet and fruity?"

He spent a moment sizing me up. "I think I've got just the thing."

I watched him pour, simply and efficiently, no tricks or showing off, which I appreciated. He passed me the drinks and I slid him a twenty.

"Thanks, and keep the change."

He rewarded me with a smile that told me I'd be well taken care of the for the rest of the night. I made my way back to Dana, handing her glass over.

"He's something, isn't he?" She winked lasciviously. "Did you ask for his number?"

"No. I asked for our drinks."

"The two aren't mutually exclusive you know! You could have asked for both."

"Nope. Not my style."

"The night is young, who knows what will happen before you head home?"

We giggled together and spent some time catching up. She introduced me to the other guests as they arrived, some of whom I had met before and others I hadn't. One friend showed up with an extra guest in tow.

"Jenna, this is Lacey and?"

"Hi Jenna, nice to meet you. This is my brother Alex. He just moved back to town and I thought he'd enjoy meeting some people."

Alex shook my hand, hanging onto it for a few seconds longer than necessary. "It's so nice to meet you."

I could see Dana watching us out of the corner of my eye, a little smirk playing on her lips.

"Thanks for coming, Alex." She drew his attention for a second.

"Thanks for having me, Dana. Happy birthday." He turned his million-dollar grin her way. "Can I buy you a birthday drink?"

She glanced down at the nearly empty glass in her hand and grinned. "Why not, thank you. I'm not driving tonight. Surprise me with something different."

"You got it. And for you?" he asked, turning my way.

"I'm good, thank you. I *do* have to drive myself home tonight."

"How about a soda then?"

Pursing my lips, I considered it as Dana turned to chat with the woman on her other side. "Alright. How about Shirley Temple please?"

He looked a little confounded at my choice but didn't make any comments. I just sat quietly as he turned to make his way to the bar. The bartender took his order and looked my way as he made the drinks. Our eyes met across the bar, and I gave him a wink. He returned the gesture and added a little paper umbrella to my soda, earning himself a genuine smile.

My drink returned and Dana did a double-take when she saw it. Cassie and I always got them whenever we weren't having alcohol. It was somewhat of our tradition. She threw her arm around my shoulder in a one-armed hug.

Raising her glass, she clinked it against mine. "To Cassie. We miss you so."

"That we do, my friend. That we do." The sentiment brought peace instead of sharp pain, knowing we had acknowledged her in a small way. She would never be forgotten.

Quite a few people made it out to celebrate with us, and eventually, trays of appetizers began appearing from the kitchen. Buffalo wings. Fried mozzarella sticks. Nachos with everything. The food just kept coming.

I looked at Dana. "Are you expecting more people?"

She giggled a tipsy giggle. "Nope. I couldn't decide. Something has to mop up all this liquor people are consuming! Eat up!"

I grabbed a plate and some munchies to nibble on,

before sliding back into my booth to resume people watching. The crowds had swelled to about capacity, the music played and people packed the dance floor. Alex had asked me to dance twice, but I just didn't feel up to it. I'd never gone out and actually danced without Cassie. At least, not that I could remember. And while I felt good about my choice to come out tonight, being here was as far I planned to go.

I made my way back to the bar for one last soda before heading home. The hunky bartender smiled at me.

"I was beginning to think you weren't going to make it back up here before you left for the night. Always sending someone else to grab you a drink, you make a guy think you're avoiding him."

I couldn't help but laugh. "Not hardly. I'm here now."

"Same thing?"

I nodded and watched him grab what he needed from behind the bar. Expertly made with another umbrella in the glass, I handed over a ten-dollar bill, but he waved it off.

"No charge. But, if you'd like to leave your number

on this napkin as a tip, I wouldn't refuse to take that." He winked at me as he slid a pen my way.

Blushing, I took the pen from his hand and stared at the napkin for a moment. I must have come across as conflicted because he waved his hand to get my attention.

"You don't have to. I don't want to come across as sleazy. You're beautiful, and you look like you'd be a lot of fun, that's all. If you want to say no, no hard feelings. And the soda is still on me."

I shook my head. "No, I want to," I said, surprising myself. "I just don't get out much and you caught me by surprise. "

I wrote my name and number on the napkin, sliding it back across the bar. He glanced down at it, then met my eyes as he stuffed it in his pocket.

"Nice to meet you Jenna. I'm Carter."

"Nice to meet you too, Carter."

Returning to the table Dana caught me and waggled her eyebrows. "Gotcha, didn't he?"

"I gave him my number; we'll see if he makes use of it."

"Oh, he will. I have no doubt."

Once I finished my drink I gathered my purse and stood. I'd had about all the being out in public I could take. Hugging Dana one more time, I glanced at the bar, planning to wave goodbye, but Carter was nowhere in sight. Surprised to feel a smidge disappointed, I wished Dana happy birthday one last time and headed to my car.

Chapter Four

The next couple of weeks passed uneventfully. I held myself accountable and worked my weekdays, leaving the weekends for other things. Some days were easier than others, which I assumed to be par for the course when you lose someone close to you.

Carter from the bar never called, leaving me annoyed with myself for looking forward to it. I hadn't even heard from Brandon aside from a text or two, and loneliness had started to set in.

With my twenty-seventh birthday looming just days

away, I began to feel more than a little mopey and sorry for myself. Friday afternoon, I logged off my work computer and sat staring out at the sky.

My phone dinged to announce a text message, catching me by surprise.

Breakfast again tomorrow?

Staring at it for a moment, I realized just how much I had missed him and Toby. This stretch of time had been the longest I had gone without seeing them since the funeral. While it might mean things could be on their way to getting back to a new normal, I needed their presence.

Definitely. What time? I'll bring the food.

Near Brandon's old place my favorite taco truck also made breakfast burritos. It sounded amazing.

Whenever you are up and ready to head over. We'll be here and I'll have coffee on.

He followed his text with a smiley face, and a shot of Toby.

Perfect. See you in the morning. Tell Toby I've missed him.

…and what am I, chopped liver?

I couldn't resist actually laughing out loud. I

realized it made me feel a little better that he had missed me too.

Don't worry, I missed you too. See you tomorrow.

I could picture him laughing at me, and hoped that he had been laughing more lately. We both needed that.

I piddled around my condo for the rest of the afternoon, fussing with the few potted plants I had on my back patio and the single living arrangement I had brought home from Cassie's memorial. I had to squash a sudden urge to go to town and buy things to redecorate the entire place. All of a sudden I wanted things to be new and fresh and different.

Settling onto the couch I decided to be content with scouring the internet for one of the hammock chairs I had always wanted to hang on the patio. Declaring it a birthday present to myself I clicked the checkout button on my digital shopping cart and it began the journey to its new home.

After pondering my choice for a minute I went back to the same site and ordered a second one. Eventually, I would have someone in my life that would be here on a regular basis and I told myself I needed them to have a chair as well.

Falling down the rabbit hole of online shopping, I perused website after website, not realizing how late it had gotten until my stomach started growling. Thankful for a freezer stuffed with various microwave dinners, I kept shopping until the timer went off and I could carry my food back to the couch. Netflix documentaries and TV dinners, what a life I lived.

My sleep could be described as restless at best that night, as I tossed and turned and dreamed of strange things. My subconscious created a string of mental images that made little sense to me, showing me things I didn't completely understand.

I saw Toby chasing tiny little raccoon babies who were not afraid of him. Carter from the bar sitting in an airplane. Lastly Brandon and I sat ensconced in my new hammock chairs. We sat on my back patio but saw Cassie's back yard view, pond and all. Weird.

Waking up left me with more questions than anything, and I continued trying to analyze my dreams as I showered and got ready for the day. Shaking my head and muttering to myself to leave it alone, as they were just dreams after all, I grabbed my keys and headed out to get breakfast.

Deciding that burritos weren't enough, I swung by the bakery in town.

"Francesca! Good morning. How have you been?"

Francesca made the best baked goods I'd ever had. We all loved to come and get treats from her, probably more often than was good for our teeth-or our waistlines.

"Jenna, darling. I've missed your face. I've been good. How about you?"

We chatted as she filled a box with our usual favorites. All I had to tell her was who would be eating them with me and she knew exactly what to pack. She even baked all-natural biscuits for pets and Toby always got a couple with every order we placed.

She looked at me soberly when I told her I was taking breakfast to Brandon. "How is he doing?"

I sighed. "Seems to be doing okay. This will actually be the first time I have seen him in a couple of weeks. Toby still looks for her, even though I know he knows she is gone. But then again, so do I. I think things are starting to heal in small ways and life is resuming a little bit of its daily flow."

"That's good to hear. I haven't seen him since the

memorial service, and I didn't want to overstep my bounds and call. I don't even know if he still has the landline hooked up."

I paused, thinking. "I don't know either. I'll ask him today. And it wouldn't be overstepping to call. Cassie loved you and he would be touched that you were thinking of him, I'm sure."

Her relief showed on her face. "Good. I will do that sometime next week then. Take your goodies, they're on me today, just because I am so happy you came in!"

"You don't have-"

She waved my disagreement away with a fluttering hand. "Shush. Take them. Have a fantastic day, and don't wait so long to come back again, promise?"

Grinning, I promised to come back soon and stuck a twenty-dollar bill in her tip jar on my way out. That woman was a gem.

I pulled into the driveway and balanced all the food on one arm as I gathered my bag and keys. Thank goodness he had agreed to do coffee or I would have had to make two trips just to get everything in the house. Cassie had had an espresso machine buried in her cupboards, although she rarely used it. Brandon had discovered it and become quite good at making lattes and cappuccinos.

Toby signaled my arrival leaving me no need to ring the bell and Brandon had the door open for me before I made it up the front steps.

"You stopped by the bakery! How did you know I have been craving Francesca's baking?"

The pretty purple box gave it away so I couldn't deny my own sweet tooth.

"I couldn't help it. Baking is something I cannot do and I realized on the way here that I could really do with some of her delectable scones, among other things."

"Come in, let's get settled. I'll make your coffee."

I grabbed plates and utensils as he made my mocha, knowing at this point just how I liked it. A twenty ounce, double shot, french vanilla mocha with whipped cream. The tall ceramic mugs were exactly the right size.

I gave Toby loves after depositing everything on the kitchen table and he licked my face, whining as if to tell me how much he missed me.

"I know, I missed you too boy." He settled down as I got his burrito out, cut it up and put it in his bowl. He always got food when we did. Spoiled boy.

Coffees finished and Toby fed, we settled down at the table to have our own meal, making idle chit chat as we did. I jumped in surprise when my phone dinged with a text message. I dug through my bag to see who could possibly be texting me on a Saturday morning. Most people I knew were not early birds.

Hey there. It's Carter, from the bar. Sorry it took me so long to text. I had a family emergency, but I wanted you to know that I do plan to use your number and I will call you soon.

I stared at my phone. Wow. The first person I had given my number to in ages and he actually contacted me. Weird.

I hope everything is okay. Talk to you soon.

"Everything alright?" Brandon looked at me with some concern. "You seem befuddled."

I glanced up at him. "Yeah, sorry. I just..." All of a sudden I felt weird telling him about it. Then I shook my head and mentally gave myself a shake. It's not like it was a secret. "A couple of weeks ago I gave my phone number to the bartender when I went out for Dana's birthday. I'd mostly given up on him and here he is sending me a text. Just caught me by surprise."

He raised his eyebrows a bit. "Why are you surprised? You gave him your number. It would make sense that he would contact you."

"Well, it's been two weeks and I figured if he hadn't called me by now he just wasn't going to, I guess. I'm out of practice. I can't remember the last time I gave a stranger my phone number."

"Did he say why he hasn't called before now?"

"Family emergency."

Brandon shrugged. "Give him the benefit of the doubt this first time. If it keeps happening block his number."

I laughed. "So easy."

"Speaking of birthdays, what do you have planned for yours next week?"

My shoulders slumped. "Nothing. I think I am just going to ignore it this year."

He reached out and touched my arm. "She wouldn't want that. You know that."

I let the tears fall. "I'm sorry. I just..."

I felt like an idiot crying in front of him over this. Yes, she had been my best friend. But this poor man had lost his wife. Who was I to put him in a place where he felt obligated to comfort me?

"Don't apologize. I get it. Trust me, boy do I get it. I still have moments where it hits me like a ton of bricks and all I can do is sit there and let it run its course. You guys were friends for two *decades* and..."

"Stop! Oh my gosh! That makes me sound SO old. I shouldn't be old enough to measure *anything* in decades yet."

He met my eyes with a grin. "Please. A decade is only ten years, and we all know you wouldn't want to go back to being ten."

"If it would bring her back..."

"But it won't. I'm struggling to accept it too. But the only way I am making it through each day is to be tough on myself. She. Is. Gone. And if I keep wallowing in it she will come back here and haunt me forever. She will do the same thing if she knows I'm letting you do it. Her only concern at the end was that we not grieve for too long. She must have asked me to promise her a hundred thousand times."

"Me too." I sniffled at the memory. Her voice had gotten so soft at the end. You could barely hear her unless you were close. But her focus, even at that point, had been on us.

"It's okay to cry. Just don't get lost in it and remember how happy she made us. I keep telling myself to be thankful for the time I was granted with her, not bitter about the time that got taken away."

His voice trailed off at the end. I met his eyes and reached out to grab his hand.

"Thank you. I needed that."

He squeezed my hand gently. "We'll both take turns needing a kick in the ass, I'm sure. She knew it too, and that's why she was so glad we'd have each other to get through this. And for that, I thank you. As understanding as everyone else is about the situation, I know you get it. And that helps me immensely. I appreciate that you come spend time with Toby and I."

"I need you guys too."

We sat in silence for a minute, then Brandon reached for the pastry box. "So, what did you bring us? I need sugar."

I laughed, letting him turn the conversation and brighten the mood. Thankfully he didn't bring my birthday up again. Cassie and I had always planned something special for each other's birthday, every year, and I planned to sit at home and drink wine alone this year. I didn't want that interrupted.

"Everything. Francesca asked how you were doing. Once she knew where I was bringing them she made sure your favorites were in there. The couple wrapped in the corner are ones she says you can freeze for later if you want, but she would prefer you just make a trip down to see her and get fresh ones whenever you feel like having one."

He took a bite and sighed. "I can't believe I haven't been down there."

"Time to make it a regular thing again."

"Mm-hmm." He couldn't speak around his mouthful of scone.

Toby whined, reminding me he hadn't gotten his biscuit yet. "Oh, and she sent half a dozen biscuits for Toby as well." I handed him one, and he took it to the corner too much on it happily.

We spent the rest of the morning just being lazy and snacking on pastries. He took me out to the tree to see if we could see the raccoon babies, but it had gotten too late in the day and they were tucked into bed until nightfall.

"Has Toby gotten used to them yet?"

"Nah. Bert and Ernestine still tease him mercilessly. They stay just out of reach."

"Poor Toby." I laughed.

"Yeah, poor dog." Brandon's sarcasm was tempered by a grin. "Somehow I don't think his incessant barking is as annoying to him as is it to me."

"I bet you're right."

We wandered back into the house. I helped put the leftovers and pastries away for later. As everything finished up, I looked around. I still had moments where being here without her weirded me out. Like I expected her to come walking down the hallway any second.

Brandon must have noticed how still I became because he stopped what he was doing too.

"I do the same thing. Like maybe she's just in the other room."

I looked over at him, semi-surprised he knew exactly what my thoughts were. "Yeah, I suppose we will be doing that for a while still."

He nodded. "What are your plans for the rest of the weekend? Going to call your new friend?"

I shook my head. "He said he is out of town with

some sort of a family emergency. He'll call me when he gets back."

Brandon raised his brows. "Okay then. He'd better. He'd be crazy not to."

Laughing, I shrugged. "He wouldn't be the first guy to not call."

Brandon wrapped me in a hug. "Thanks for coming, and if you need someone to keep you company just call."

"Thanks. I will. You can always call me too. Take care and I'm sure I'll see you soon."

Stroking Toby's head softly, I kissed him goodbye and headed out the door.

Chapter Five

I spent the week before my birthday doing my absolute best to keep myself occupied so I had less time to be melancholy. Scrolling through social media, I toyed with the idea of booking myself some sort of singles vacation, the kind where you weren't expected to have a date for things, yet they made no effort to set you up with anyone else on the excursions either. Just single people who were okay with doing things alone, but sometimes wanted someone to do them with. Did that make any sense?

Thursday rolled around and I finished my shift early thanks to having worked right through lunch. Perusing the contents of the refrigerator left me realizing that I needed to hit the grocery store pretty badly, but I couldn't find the motivation to go. Just as I had decided to order take out, my phone dinged.

Text message. Saved by the bell.

Hey there. It's Carter. I know it's last minute, but I just got back in town. I haven't been to get groceries so I thought I would see if you wanted to go grab a bite to eat?

I laughed, thinking we might be more alike than I had first realized.

That's hilarious. I am literally standing in front of my fridge lamenting the fact that I, too, need to go to the grocery store! And welcome back, hope everything turned out ok.

I'll tell you about it over dinner. What do you feel like eating?

I couldn't decide. Part of me wanted Indian food at Cassie's favorite spot. The other part of me wasn't ready to share that pain with him yet, and I hadn't been back there since her funeral.

Can't decide. Do you have a preference?

Fate must have had nothing better to do that evening because his response included the name and address of the very restaurant I had been avoiding.

I know it. Meet you there in an hour?

I needed to fortify my defenses before heading there. Oh, and I probably needed to shower and get dressed in decent clothes as well.

Perfect. I'm looking forward to seeing you.

Me too.

I smiled. In spite of my trepidation about going to Cassie's favorite restaurant with him, I found myself being excited about the prospect of seeing him.

After showering I stood in front of the closet trying to pick out something to wear. I didn't want to go overboard since the restaurant was far from fancy, but I wanted to look nice for him.

My stomach growled during the process, reminding me to hurry the hell up and get moving. New jeans, cute top, fancy earrings. Done. Slipping on some casual shoes, I grabbed my bag and headed out the door.

I parked in the lot, taking a deep breath to steady my nerves and my emotions before getting out of the car. As I walked in the front door Carter had just given our info to the host.

"Miss Jenna, welcome back. I have not seen you in so long. How are you doing?"

I smiled. "I'm doing good, thank you."

"This is your first time back, yes?"

I nodded, not quite trusting my voice.

"Do you want your usual table, or do you want me to seat you somewhere else?"

Hesitating, I couldn't decide. Part of me wanted the old familiarity of the table by the fountain that we had always eaten at, and the other half of me wanted to be on the far side of the restaurant where I couldn't even see "our" table.

"Um..." I looked at Carter helplessly. "I'm sorry..." My voice was barely above a whisper.

"Jenna, so you want to go somewhere else? I -"

"No. No. It's okay. I promise I'll explain once we are seated. Can we have our table if it is available?"

"It is. Right this way."

The hostess led us towards the back, and my heart beat a little louder with every step we took. I sat in my usual seat and swallowed hard as I watched Carter sit in her chair.

"I'll be right back with drinks," the waitress left us after getting our beverage requests.

"Jenna..."

"I'm sorry. I thought I would do better than this. Let me explain." I took a deep breath and Carter watched me quietly. "This has always been our favorite place to eat, my best friend Cassie and I."

I paused to take a drink of water. Forcing the words out made my throat close up.

"She died last spring. Five months ago. This is the first time I've been back here since the last time we ate here together. And it turns out I'm struggling with it a little more than I had expected to. But I needed this. I'm just sorry it's on our first date. I probably should have come alone, or with Brandon for the first visit."

"Brandon? Are you seeing someone?" He seemed a little taken aback as I mentioned Brandon's name.

"What? Oh, no. Sorry." I laughed nervously. "Brandon is Cassie's husband. Was. He proposed to her right after she got her diagnosis. She had an inoperable brain tumor. Once they discovered it she only had a few weeks left."

"I'm so, so sorry." Carter's voice was filled with quiet sympathy.

"Thank you. She was an amazing person, and we had been friends most of our lives. We met in second grade and became inseparable that first day. I socked a boy in the nose because he made her cry."

Carter laughed. "Somehow I can see you doing that."

"Anyways, Brandon and I have been sort of propping each other up these last few months. Plus, we share custody of Toby."

"Toby?" Carter seemed curious.

"Yep. A gorgeous golden lab. Cassie had asked me to take him as soon as she got her diagnosis, but that was before Brandon proposed to her. Since Brandon sold his place and moved into hers, we both agreed that it would be best for Toby to stay in the place he knew as home. I get him on random weekends, and any time Brandon has to be gone for any length of time. It's working out pretty well so far."

Carter reached out and touched my hand, stopping short of actually grabbing it. "I can see you loved her very much."

I nodded, trying to blink back the tears. I hadn't spoken of Cassie with anyone that didn't already know her, so this was new territory for me. I didn't want to cry on our first date.

"Thank you for sharing this with me."

"Thank you. If I haven't scared you off yet." I raised my eyebrows in a quirky challenge.

"It will take more than a little bit of sadness to make me run away."

"I'm glad. Your turn, I hope the family emergency worked itself out?"

He took his turn frowning. "My dad had a heart attack. It was touch and go for a few days, but they did surgery and his prognosis is good. He got to go home from the hospital a couple of days ago, and when my mom insisted she would be fine taking care of him, I headed back."

"I'm sorry! But I am really glad he came through it and is getting better."

The waitress brought our drinks back and we ordered our food. For a first date, we had gotten off to a heavy start, but at least we could talk about those kinds of subjects.

The rest of the meal both of us made a conscious effort to keep things more light-hearted. We talked about our families, and where we had grown up. We discovered we had actually gone to the same middle and high school, although neither of us could remember the other. He told me he needed to get out his yearbooks and look me up. I grimaced. That made him laugh.

Before I knew it our food had long been finished and we had been sitting and chatting for two hours. Seeing what time it was surprised me.

"Wow. You must be easy to talk to. I can't believe how much time has gone by."

"Right back atcha. This is one of the most pleasant nights I have had in a really long time."

We stood and he grabbed the check right out from under me.

"What do I owe?"

"Nothing. My treat."

"Thank you. And thanks for being understanding about how weird I acted."

"You didn't act weird. I thought you handled it really well. I'm thankful that you chose to open up to me and tell me about her."

"Well, if you end up sticking around you'll hear a lot more about her. You'll probably get tired of hearing me talk about her."

"Never. What's important to you is important to me."

My insides got all warm and squishy at the thought of having someone in my life who truly valued the things I did. So far Carter seemed like a guy who might be worth putting some effort into. Only time would tell.

He walked me to my car, only to discover we were larked right next to each other.

"Well, isn't this convenient?"

I held my keys as I turned to say goodnight. "Thank you so much, again, for a lovely evening."

"Thank you. Can I call you so we can do it again soon?"

"I have to say I would be mighty disappointed if you didn't."

He leaned in, kissing me gently on the cheek. "Get in, and lock your doors. Safety first."

I followed his instructions, and he moved out of the way so I could back out of the parking spot. Turning, I waved to him as he stood with his car door open, watching me drive out of the lot.

For the short drive home my thoughts were occupied with the potential of this first date. Carter seemed like a really nice guy, and a gentleman as well. I didn't want to get too invested just yet, but the thought of this going somewhere for the long run made me smile.

Then my heart broke a little as I realized I couldn't call Cassie up and share it with her. There would never be double dates with her and Brandon, and we'd never have kids together that would grow up and be best friends also.

Parking my car in the garage, I hit the button to close the door behind me just as I noticed something small scoot across the driveway and slip under the closing door. Surprised, I got out of my car and looked around. At first, I didn't see anything, but scratching in the far corner gave me a clue.

I slipped around the car slowly, not wanting to scare whatever it was. Suspecting a squirrel, I had almost decided to go back around and reopen the door to let it escape when I heard a small meow. A kitten? Oh boy. Now I would have to find out who it belonged to.

"Here kitty kitty..." I bent over to look beneath the bench and saw a pair of tiny green eyes staring back at me. "Aw..."

I reached out slowly, trying not to frighten it. After some convincing it came out from around the box it hid behind at launched itself at me. The poor thing looked way too little to be away from its mama, much less out roaming the big wide world by itself.

Tucking it into my arm, we headed in the house. I pulled up our neighborhood group on social media and posted to see if anyone was missing a kitten. In the meantime, the little thing needed some food and water.

Stumped for the moment, seeing as how I didn't keep random cans of cat food on hand, I opened up a can of Toby's food that I kept in the pantry and scooped a little into a bowl. It might not be cat food, but the poor thing didn't care. It wolfed the entire serving right down, and looked at me expectantly for more.

"Sorry, little one. I don't need you puking on my floor. In a little bit."

Keeping one eye on the kitten, I dug out the card for Toby's vet and made a call for advice. While I love the vet's office, the on-call service is minimal, and their advice didn't help me much. She basically told me that if I didn't find the owners and decided to keep the little thing to bring it into the office for a checkup and shots. Huh?

Realizing I also didn't want any kitty accidents on my floor, I picked the little ball of fluff up and headed out the front door. Assuming it hadn't gotten far on its own, it must belong to one of the neighbors in the complex.

Chapter Six

Almost ninety minutes later I had met most of the neighbors in my complex and I still had possession of one tiny kitten. Sighing, I put some food and water in the spare bathroom and, after picking up all the linens in the room, headed to the store to get some things to tide us over until I found its home.

I stood in the pet aisle pondering my choices when I heard a familiar voice.

"Fancy seeing you here."

I spun around, to find Carter standing four feet

away, his grocery cart indicating he had done most of his shopping already.

"Hey! Long time no see."

"Had I known you were going to be here to we could have extended our date."

"I wouldn't have been here actually, but when I got home a tiny kitten decided my place made a good hideout and I don't have anything to take care of him. Her. It. I don't know if it's a boy or a girl."

"Are you keeping it?"

"Gosh, no. I spent over an hour checking with my neighbors and none of them claimed it, so I will be looking for its owners more tomorrow. Until then I don't want it going to the bathroom on my floor, or starving to death, so here I am."

He looked pointedly at the small package of furry mice in my hand. "It looks to me like you're settling in for the long haul."

"No. I just don't want the little thing to be bored. Bored animals destroy stuff."

Carter laughed. "I bet you the next time I call you to ask you out you still have the kitten."

I raised my eyebrows. "Oh yeah? And what are we

betting?"

"Loser buys dinner at the winner's choice of restaurant."

"Deal." I stuck my hand out, then snatched it back before we could shake on it. "But no cheating. You can't call me later tonight or tomorrow to ask me out again."

He laughed a deep belly laugh, and stuck his hand out. "Deal. Can I call you tomorrow to talk to you though?"

"Hmm..." I teased him, pretending to try and decide whether to let him call me.

He pouted an over-exaggerated pout, pretending to be hurt that I didn't immediately say yes. Relenting, I nodded.

"Good. Now pick out all the things you need for your new kitty." He started grabbing food, treats, toys and other necessities and throwing them in my cart.

"Wait! Stop! I only need the bare minimum. It will only be here for a couple of days at the most."

He looked me in the eye. "I don't believe you. In fact, I am so certain you'll be keeping it, I will pay you back for everything you buy tonight, even your groceries, if you don't."

"You are a little bit of a gambler, aren't you? I'm sensing you might have a bit of an issue." I made sure to smile as I said it, so he'd know I only teased. I figured he might as well get used to the fact that I can be a sarcastic bitch from the beginning.

My heart fluttered when he took the bait and teased me right back. "More bets? Wanna bet a trip to Vegas on it? There's plenty of gambling there. And I'm just that sure I've got you pegged."

"Let's stick with dinner and groceries for now. Once I can be certain you aren't a poor loser we'll up the ante a little."

He laughed. "Sounds practical to me. I have to go pay for my groceries before my ice cream melts. I'll talk to you soon!"

I watched him walk away, admiring his backside in his jeans, before returning my attention back to the kitten supplies. I put everything he had picked out back on the shelf. Then, going through my mental checklist I grabbed a kitty box and litter, a bag of dry food and a couple cans of wet. I threw the tiny mice in there because I really didn't want the little bugger to decide to use his claws on my furniture. And just in case it didn't like the mice I grabbed a multi-pack of other toys. You know, to save my furniture.

I moved through the rest of my grocery shopping fairly quickly, certain I would be back to pick up all the things I forgot since I dared to shop without a list. Remembering our little bet, I threw a few extra things in there that I might not have normally bought for myself, just to teach him a lesson. After all, my birthday was in two days and I deserved a little something special.

After dragging my purchases in from the garage I opened the bathroom door to check on my unexpected guest and get the litter box set up. To my surprise there didn't seem to be any damage. The little critter acted happy to see me, rubbing against my ankles and purring. I picked it up and gave it some pets. The poor thing had gotten lost and most likely missed its family, some affection was the least I could do for it.

I took an old towel and made a little bed in the corner, then headed out to put groceries away. Making sure it had a bowl full of water I grabbed another bowl to give dry food in. Grabbing a place mat from the drawer I put both bowls in the corner, where I hopefully wouldn't trip over them.

Kittens make for curious creatures, and I had to consistently watch to be sure it didn't get shut in a cupboard or drawer. I doled the toys I purchased out one at a time and managed to make them last all of fifteen minutes. The kitten had all of them before I got all the groceries put away. Shrugging, I decided it didn't matter that much.

By the time I needed to head to bed the kitten had worn itself out. Gathering a few of the toys I headed to put it in the bathroom for the night. The little rascal had other ideas though and took off down the hallway. I had to wonder if it knew it was about to be confined again.

Following it down the hallway I peeked in my room to see if it had gone in there and, sure enough, I saw it curled up on my bed, right on the pillow no less.

"Oh no you don't. You are sleeping in the bathroom."

Picking it up I took it and the toys to its room for the night. I set it on the towel and tucked one of the mice in next to it. Attempting to beat it out the door I realized I couldn't leave the poor thing locked in there all night without food and water. Sighing I headed for the kitchen to grab the bowls. The second I opened the door the sneaky little one escaped right through my legs and took off like a shot back towards my room.

I looked at the litter box in the bathroom, thought of the bowls in the kitchen, and sighed. Back in my room the fur-ball had returned to the pillow and curled up to go to sleep. At least it wasn't trying to take over my side.

I completed my bedtime routine and looked over at my new (temporary) roommate. It really was adorable. Hopefully, I'd find his or her family tomorrow, otherwise, I might be in danger of losing a bet.

Morning brought me a case of disorientation as I woke to feeling my head vibrating and wondering if I'd developed a fever overnight. It turns out that my new little buddy had chosen to ensconce him or herself on the pillow directly above my head and purr its heart out.

Reaching out, I grabbed it gently and attempted to remove it. The sharp claws got tangled in my hair and I spent a minute or two untangling us from each other. Once successful I settled the kitten next to me instead of on top of me. It continued to purr and rub against me as I pet it.

Having never been much of a cat person I found myself oddly accepting of the idea that I may not find a family missing it and therefore I could subsequently adopt it. However, the notion that losing a bet to Carter seemed just as acceptable alarmed me.

I checked my email and social media for any responses to my lost kitten ads and found nothing. Sighing, I called the vets office and made an appointment for the last slot of the day. If I didn't find anyone claiming to be the owner, I would be taking it to get shots and a checkup. And then texting Carter to tell him he won the bet after all.

Reminding myself that I didn't need to keep the kitten just to have an excuse to call him, I dug deep into my real feelings. Loneliness had set in with Cassie's loss and I needed to remediate somehow. Since I barely had the willpower to go out in public and meet any more people right now, perhaps a pet made the perfect starting place. Toby would acclimate and perhaps they could be the best of friends when he did visit.

Once ready for the day I put the cat into the bathroom and drove around the neighboring areas to see if anyone had posted signs looking for a lost kitten. I grabbed coffee while I was out, because why not?

Seeing none, I returned home to get a few hours of

work in before the trip to the vet needed to be made. The tiny kitten shot out the bathroom door as soon as I opened it, meowing as if offended that I had dared to lock up and leave the house.

As I worked in my office the hours flew by and I spent more time trying to keep the kitten from making a disaster of my desk than I did actually working. Once I'd hit the minimum allowable hours for the shift I gave up, logged off, and settled onto the couch with a snack. With a purring ball of fur in my lap I pondered the fact that I had hit my last day of being twenty-six. Tomorrow when I woke up I'd be twenty-seven.

And Cassie wouldn't be here. She'd never be here to celebrate my birthday again. Instead of trying to curb the tears as I usually did, this time I just let them flow. Reduced to a blubbering, soggy mess, even the kitten decided my mood was above its pay grade and took off to hide in parts of the house that didn't include getting cried on.

Lamenting the guilt of being the one healthy and alive, I cried for all the things she would miss. Then I cried for all of the things in my life that I would have to weather without her. As the headache settled into my frontal lobe, I realized that I had to be out the door to the vet's office soon, and I looked a wreck.

Quickly showering and hoping it would wash the worst of the evidence away, I dressed and then tried to repair the damage with whatever makeup I had. (My success was limited.)

I walked through the house looking for the kitten, calling "Here, kitty kitty," to no avail.

Panic grew as I double-checked each door and window to be sure there had been no path to the outdoors for it to escape via. Nothing. Getting desperate I opened a can of wet food, hoping the sound or smell would entice it from its hiding place.

It worked, though barely. Tiny padded feet snuck down the hallway, looking for danger before poking its head into the kitchen.

"There you are!"

Picking it up and giving it a snuggle, I apologized for scaring it. Then mentally berated myself. I hadn't gotten a carrier while out the other night. How did I get it to the vet without losing it? A search of my closet turned up a mesh beach bag with a solid bottom. Shrugging, I stuck a towel in the bottom and slid the wriggling cat in, zipping it to prevent escape. It would have to do.

The piteous meows that it made all the way to the vet's office almost gave me second thoughts about whether a kitten was for me. Reminding myself that the poor thing just didn't know any other way to express what was most likely fear, I talked in a quiet voice the rest of the way, which calmed it some.

Arriving at the office to check in the receptionist wanted all sorts of information that I had to explain I didn't have.

"I don't even know if it's a boy or a girl," I confessed.

She just smiled. "That's okay darling, we can enter this information after you've seen the doctor. Go ahead and take a seat and someone will call you back shortly."

Taking my beach bag and purse I found a spot on one of the hard plastic chairs the kept us out of the way of the other critters also waiting their turn. The poor cat had begun shaking with the onslaught of all the new sounds and smells.

Thinking I would comfort it I took it out of the bag and attempted to snuggle it in my arms. Unfortunately, I didn't account for its desire to run and hide, and the second that zipper opened the poor thing took off like a shot.

Bleeding from the scratches on my arm I called out, and jumped out of the chair. The pups next to me took the running as an invitation to chase and pulled their poor unsuspecting owner to the floor. Apologizing as I headed down the hallway to save the poor baby from its own bad choices, I stopped and looked around when I didn't see hide nor hair of it.

The dogs had stopped too, confused, which allowed their owner to get a hold of the leashes once more.

"I am so sorry." I cringed. "I've never had a cat and I didn't even think that it might run off. Are you okay?"

"Don't worry about it. I'm fine. Where did you get the kitten? It looked awfully small."

"It ran into my garage as I pulled in the other night. I canvased the neighborhood but it doesn't seem to belong to anybody. So here I am, just making sure it's okay."

"Cats have tendency to choose their family, so congratulations on your new fur-baby."

I laughed. "I am about to lose a bet over this. I

swore I wouldn't keep it."

It was her turn to laugh. "Some things are just out of your control."

She returned to the waiting room with her pups and I looked around the limited options for the kitten to be hiding. Peeking into a slightly open door, I found it, snuggling with the doctor at the desk.

"I'm so sorry. I didn't think it would run off."

He shook his head. "No worries. Let's move to the exam room across the hall and we can get the appointment started."

He led the way, still holding the escapee, and I followed meekly behind, my ears still burning from letting a less-than-two-pound creature get the drop on me.

He shut the door, presumably to prevent any more escapades and set the kitten on the exam table. He began by giving it a quick once over.

"Seems quite young to be away from its mother."

I shared the story of how it had come to take refuge in my garage, as well as admitting I didn't even know whether to call it a he or she. A quick check and the doctor settled that for me.

"It's definitely a girl. She looks to only be about five or six weeks, by my best guess. Is she eating solid food?"

"Yes," I answered and listed off what I had bought during my late evening run to the store.

"Excellent." He proceeded to take her temperature, check her teeth and feel her belly. "Overall she seems very healthy. I will give her some dewormer just to be safe, but I don't recommend starting her shots for at least another two weeks. We'll deworm her again at that appointment, since we don't know what, if any, veterinary care she has had up to this point. You do plan on keeping her?"

I sighed. "Yes. If her family doesn't show up looking to claim her."

"Okay, we will get her set up with all the appointment she needs for routine care and to get her spayed. Do you have any questions?"

"Well, as dumb as this sounds, I have never had a cat before. I know nothing about them. So is there anything I should know in general. Like, obvious things that people should know but I probably don't?"

"They are pretty self-sufficient. Do you plan to let

her go outdoors?" I shook my head. "Okay then not too much to worry about. We can microchip her when we do the spay and I will have Betty at the front desk give you some basic care sheets."

"Thank you so much for getting me in and taking a look at her."

"No problem, we'll see you in a couple weeks."

I paid for the visit and collected the printed sheets from the front desk. On my way out the lady with the pups smiled at me.

"They're always worth losing the bet over." She winked.

I waved, and nodded in agreement.

Chapter Seven

During the drive home I kept glancing over at the tiny calico kitten, now sleeping peacefully in my beach bag. I wanted to honor Cassie in some way, but not actually name the cat after her. That would have felt a little odd.

I decided to drive through and picked up take out as my pre-birthday dinner, ensuring I wouldn't have to cook or clean up after the meal. As I pulled into the lot my phone dinged.

If I promise not to collect on the bet yet, do you

want to have dinner with me?

Laughing at his qualification of not negating the bet, I pulled into a parking spot to respond.

I'm just picking up Chinese take-out. Join me at my place?

Normally I would not invite someone I had just met to my place, or even told them where I lived to be picked up for a date, but I instinctively trusted Carter. Now to hope my gut hadn't misled me.

He responded affirmatively and I sent my address, letting him know I'd be home in about ten minutes.

Perfect. I'll get there in about half an hour. See you soon.

The sudden realization that I should have told him it would take me longer to get home so that I would have time to get ready had me stepping on the gas pedal a little harder than necessary. I wanted to at least freshen up, although I suppose the old adage of what you see is what you get applied in this case. I wouldn't always be putting for the extra effort to be pretty for him...

I set the take out on the table and released the as-yet-unnamed kitten on the floor for her to do her thing as I headed in to at least look in the mirror. Tossing my hair in a quick bun left me just enough time to slap a little mascara on when I heard the doorbell ring.

That had to have been less than thirty minutes.

Picking up the kitten to prevent her from running out when I opened the front door, I opened the door wide and welcomed him in.

"Come in, it's good to see you."

He held up a bottle of wine. "I come bearing gifts. I see you are becoming accustomed to your tiny temporary roommate?"

Biting my tongue to hold back the laughter, I tried to look haughty. "There's no point in being mean to the poor creature."

"Uh-huh. Gotcha." The wry turn of his lips more than telegraphed his opinion on the subject. Words would have been superfluous.

Setting her on the floor once she had no chance of escape, we headed to the dining room, attempting to keep from tripping as the kitten ran amongst our feet.

The assortment of take out boxes lay spread out on the counter, and I handed him a plate and some silverware as I grabbed glasses for the wine.

"Wanna eat out here, or watch some TV and eat on

the couch?"

Seeing as how I lived alone, I usually only ate at the dining room table if I was working on something requiring the surface, or I had company over. My coffee table in the living room actually pulled up to a tabletop so you could eat comfortably without hunching over your food.

"We could eat out there and try to find a movie to watch?"

"Excellent. This way." I grabbed my plate and glass, tucking the wine bottle under my arm.

As soon as we settled on the couch the kitten insisted on knowing what we were doing. She wound her way between us, attempting to get on the table and help herself to our food.

"No. No. Bad kitty. Chinese food is for humans." Lifting her up, I settled her into the corner of the couch, nestled against my leg, where she gave up and decided to fall asleep.

Carter laughed. "I don't see how you can claim you don't want to keep it."

"It's a her."

He raised his eyebrows in question, not uttering a

word.

"Gah, okay okay. I took her to the vet today. She needed a checkup and I wanted to be sure there wasn't anything wrong with her."

"Yeah? What's her name?"

"I haven't decided yet." My hands raised in defeat. "You were right. Unless somebody shows up to claim her she'll become a permanent resident."

"Cats make good companions. I think it's great."

He didn't mention the bet at all, raising my impression of him even higher.

"I want to honor Cassie in some way, but not actually name the cat after her, that would be strange."

"Hm. Did she have a nickname at all? Or a favorite flower?"

"No nickname. She liked lilacs, but that doesn't fit. I think I will just have to get to know her personality a little better as we spend more time together and then something will hopefully jump out at me. I can't keep calling her kitty forever."

"Well, I mean, you *could* I suppose."

"Yes, I *could*, smart ass, but I don't want to."

"Well, those are two different scenarios entirely.

Not being able to and not wanting to are not the same thing."

"Well, sir, thank you for that explanation. I don't know what poor little ole me would have done without you here to make sure I understood." I laced my fake southern accent with sarcasm as heavy as it would go.

"Yes, ma'am, glad to be of service ma'am." He pretended to tip his nonexistent hat my direction and I responded by threatening him with my chopstick.

We laughed together as I popped a dumpling in my mouth. It felt fantastic to kick back and relax and be able to laugh without feeling the sorrow that had been plaguing me for months. The wine probably helped, but I had no doubt that my current company had a whole lot to do with it too.

The television stayed off, we just ate and chatted, talking about our careers and our families. It turned out bartending was just a part-time temporary job that he did because he enjoyed it, and it gave him extra money for things he wanted. Hours flew by, and before we knew it we were closing in on midnight.

"I'd better get home, and let you get to bed. Can I help you clean up?"

"I'll get it, thank you for offering though. Let me walk you out."

We headed down the front hall, and he grabbed his jacket from the hook near the door. All of a sudden the hall didn't seem wide enough for the both of us, and I realized just how close together we stood. Out height difference meant I craned my neck to look up at him, and I wondered if he would kiss me.

"Thank you for coming over. And for the wine. I had a fantastic time." My voice trailed off as I finished the sentence.

"Thanks for having me; I had a great time too."

He pulled me into a hug and I wrapped my arms around him, leaning into his arms. As we separated he leaned over, planting a soft kiss on my forehead.

"Let's do it again soon?"

"Yes, please."

"I'll call you." He waved as he slipped out the front door, thankfully before I could get my voice in working order and ask him to stay.

I peeked out the window as he pulled out of the driveway, watching his tail lights until he turned out of the complex and onto the main road. He'd left the bottle of wine we hadn't opened for me, and I decided to go ahead and have another glass. After all, it would be my birthday in less than an hour.

Glass in hand, I settled on the couch, covering with one of the blankets I kept in the living room. My new friend gave her stamp of approval and settled into my lap, purring like crazy.

"What are we going to call you, little one? You need a name."

Eyes closed, she didn't acknowledge my voice at, uncaring if I called her anything at all. The gentle rumbling in her chest was soothing to my strange mood. Partially melancholy, and partially excited at what lay on the horizon. Carter had reminded me that I wanted to have companionship in my life too.

Imagining what Cassie would say if she were here, I chuckled out loud. No doubt about it, she would have been encouraging me from the beginning. She probably would have given him my phone number before he ever asked for it. That's the kind of friend she had been.

When her and Brandon had first started dating she claimed to know for a fact that it wouldn't turn into anything serious, and I should feel free to "take a stab it." That's exactly how she worded it as if dating was a skill to be attempted. I teased her about it mercilessly as they continued to date in spite of her original opinion of the pairing.

I must have dozed off because the next thing I knew it was going on two in the morning. I had finished the rest of the wine in my glass and wandered down memory lane. For one of the first times, I let myself remember and it didn't cause as much as pain as it had been since she died. I smiled softly. This is what she wanted for me, to think of her and smile, not cry.

I left the kitty curled up in the blanket and headed to brush my teeth before bed. By the time I finished, she had taken up on "her" pillow for the night, not to be left in the living room alone no matter how cozy the covers were.

It took me a while to fall asleep again, but when I did my dreams were pleasant and I drifted into a deeper, more restful sleep than I had enjoyed in a long time.

Chapter Eight

The morning of my birthday greeted me with gray skies, overcast and cloudy, which was par for the course in the fall. In spite of the few hours of sleep I had gotten I felt more refreshed than if I had slept a solid ten hours. Wine made for an excellent sleep aid.

I barely had coffee on when there was a knock at the door. Curious, I looked through the peephole before answering.

To my surprise, Brandon and Toby stood on the doorstep, Brandon's arms full of things. I swung open the door, forgetting to check for the kitten who made a beeline for the outside. She got nose to nose with Toby and did an about-face, streaking back down the hallway to hide. Toby took off after her like a shot.

"Toby, you be nice to the baby!" I called after him as I managed to evade being trampled. "Come in, what a great surprise."

I pulled the door to let him by, shutting securely once he was inside.

"Happy birthday!" He led the way down the hall to the dining room.

"Thank you, I'll be right back." I could hear Toby whining from my bedroom, meaning the poor cat was probably up in top of my dresser or out of reach.

"Toby. Leave it." He looked at me, not quite willing to back away just yet. "Go. Lay. Down."

Huffing, he did as he was told, although making sure I knew he didn't like it one bit.

"Here, kitty. It's okay. Come here. The doggy won't hurt you." She peered down at me balefully. Already I had offended her by letting that other creature into the house and now she wanted nothing to do with me for the moment.

Leaving her be to calm down, I pulled the door closed to keep the dog out and went to see Brandon. By the time I got out there, Toby lay in his bed in the corner and Brandon had laid out an entire breakfast spread. Burritos from my favorite taco truck, coffee from my favorite stand and pastries from Francesca's. Everything Cassie always brought for breakfast on my birthday.

"Oh my God." I tried not to cry. "You did not have to do all this. I'm speechless. Thank you so much."

He smiled a soft smile. "Oh but I did. I have my instructions."

Curious, I raised my eyebrows. He took my hand and sat me in the chair. "Take this while I get plates and silverware." He handed me an envelope, my name written on the front in printing that was as familiar to me as my own.

"Oh my..." I just stared at it for a moment. Could I open it without losing my self-control?

"I got a hand-delivered package yesterday. Her lawyer delivered it and let me know that he had been instructed to be sure I received it precisely on the day she indicated. The one for you was also in the envelope."

With trembling hands, I carefully slit the top of the envelope with the knife Brandon handed me as if he had known I wouldn't want to damage it in any way.

The birthday card read on the front "To my very best friend..." and was covered in sparkly flowers. Opening it the inside read "Sorry we couldn't celebrate together, but I hope it's the best one yet! Happy birthday!"

By that point, the tears had made it impossible to see what she had actually written, and I made use of the tissues Brandon handed me. He sat quietly after pulling up his chair close to mine.

Oh Jenna, where do I begin? First off - HAPPY BIRTHDAY! You're older than me again. This was supposed to be our twentieth year celebrating birthdays together, and I had to go and screw it up. I feel bad, so in my place, I sent the next best thing. (Hopefully, you didn't have any other plans.) I know you're crying right now, and I want you to stop it. This card was intended to make you happy. I wanted to be able to tell you happy birthday one last time. Smile as you remember all the crazy things we've done to celebrate over the years. Maybe tell Brandon about some of them – you know which ones not to mention. Wink. Wink. No matter what, always know how much I love you. I'm not gone. I will always be by your side. Love, Cassie.

"Oh my gosh... she's killing me..." The tears wouldn't stop. Looking up at Brandon I saw his eyes glisten as well, but so far he'd managed to keep them in. "Did you know she did this?"

He shook his head. "I had no idea until I opened the package last night. She wanted to be sure on your first birthday without her that not much changed." He handed me a small, gift-wrapped box. "I have instructions to give this to you also."

I shook my head, mute from the emotions. Pulling one edge of the purple ribbon, I untied it and opened the box. Nestled in the cardboard box sat another box, this time one of the velvet ones you would find from a jewelry store.

Brandon shrugged when I looked towards him. "I had absolutely nothing to do with this. I'm as mystified as you are."

The lid snapped open with a pop to reveal the most beautiful necklace. A grown-up version of a child's "best friends" necklace, the heart was cast in gold and studded with tiny gemstones. Pink for my birthday and blue for hers with little diamonds around the rest of the edge. She had given me the half that said "BEST."

I took it out of the box and stared at it silently.

"Would you like me to help you put it on?" Brandon's voice was soft.

"Yes, please." I handed it over and turned my back to him, shivering as his hands brushed my neck. I couldn't believe Cassie had done this for me. "Thank you."

"My pleasure. It looks fantastic on you."

Minutes passed as we sat in silence. Our introspection got interrupted when Toby had decided he'd been waiting long enough for his burrito and began to whine. We laughed.

"I guess we should eat before it gets cold." Toby laid his head on my thigh and looked up at me with his most pitiful face.

Brandon dug Toby's burrito out of the bag, cut it up and dumped it in his bowl. "There you go big guy. We wouldn't want you to starve to death or anything."

"I can't tell you how much I appreciate this." I looked over at him, still teary-eyed, to make sure he knew how sincerely I meant it.

"You know I would have come even without Cassie's instructions, right?" he said quietly. "You are important to me too."

Reaching over, I laid my hand on his arm. "I cannot tell you how much that means to me right now. You are so special to me too, and I remind myself regularly to try and not smother you with how needy I am."

His lips quirked up in a half-smile. "I think we both deserve to be a little needy, and who better to understand it than the person going through the exact same thing?"

"Thank you."

I leaned my head on his shoulder, and he rested his against mine. We sat like that for a moment, until he grabbed our coffees.

"Should we reheat and finish our breakfast?"

My stomach grumbled in reply. "I guess so!"

As we ate Toby slept peacefully on the floor. Until I saw him perk up and his ears rotate toward my bedroom.

"Oh man! The cat!" I stood, intending to go rescue her. "Would you keep a hold of Toby for a minute. I want to introduce you guys to someone but he needs to be patient."

"That's right, I meant to ask you about that before we got sidetracked."

I cracked the bedroom door, hoping to grab hold of her before she darted out between my feet and managed to be mostly successful. Cradling her in my arms I talked softly to her as we went back down the hallway toward the dining room.

At first sight of Toby, she hissed and attempted to jump to the floor and flee.

"Shhh... it's okay. Toby is a good boy. Aren't you Toby? No. Stay."

He whined with excitement. Brandon held him in place as I knelt on the floor and I held the kitten closer. She didn't hiss again but meowed uncomfortably. Toby whined softly, stretching his neck out to greet her. She swiped at him, causing Brandon and I to laugh at Toby's offended expression.

We spent about ten minutes letting them sniff each other, and then I let her go. She didn't run away immediately, which I took to be a good sign.

"So, how did you acquire a kitten?"

I filled him in on Dana's birthday party, the kitten scooting into the garage as I pulled in, and everything up to the bet I made with Carter.

"Ooh, you had a date..." he teased me with a smile.

"Two actually, he happened to text as I was grabbing take out last night and came over to eat with me."

"And?"

"Eh. I don't know. It's pretty new and I' not sure I'm ready for anything serious, but he seems like a nice enough guy."

"Ah, the nice guy..." He let his words trail off as he watched me carefully.

I just shrugged. "We'll see."

"Am I interrupting something then? Is he planning something special for your birthday?"

I snorted. "I didn't tell him it was my birthday. Two dates is way too soon to be sharing that kind of personal information. God forbid he feel obligated to do something for it."

"I don't know about that, but I'm glad because I thought we could hang out and then go over to Amanda and Liam's so you could meet the babies. Maybe get more take and out and take them some dinner and cake for your birthday?"

"Oh! What a fantastic idea! I just love it, thank you so much. I can't believe you are doing all this for me!"

He laughed again. "I told you I would have had my own plan even without Cassie's interference."

I giggled. "That's exactly what it is, too. She had to be sure that we did things her way, even if she couldn't be here to see it through." I took a deep breath. "God, I miss her."

His laughter quieted. "Me too. I can't believe it's almost been six months. I am making it through the days without the consistent stabbing grief most days, and I almost feel like I can breathe again."

Nodding, I told him the story of the day I found the penny, and how I had been keeping it in my pocket every day since.

"I just know it was from her. A penny that shiny and new from the year we were born? What are the odds?"

"I agree."

"Wanna see it?" I was already halfway out of my chair before he had even answered, knowing that he would, indeed, want to take a look at it.

"Of course."

"Be right back." I heard him tell Toby to stay as the

kitten followed me down the hall, not wanting to be left behind.

Grabbing it from the small dish on the bathroom counter I couldn't help but smile again at how shiny and sparkly it appeared, in spite of its age. Not that it was *that* old, of course.

I returned to the dining room and handed it over. I followed his movements as he rubbed the pad of his thumb over the copper surface.

"You're right, it looks as if it just came from the mint yesterday."

The kitten chose that moment to jump onto the table, knocking the penny out of his hand and sending it rolling.

"Ugh, kitty, NO."

He managed to snatch it before it careened off the edge and disappeared, while I picked up the kitten.

"What did you name her, anyways?"

"I didn't. I haven't come up with anything yet. I wanted to honor Cassie without actually naming the cat after her, especially since Amanda already named the baby after her. Any ideas?"

"What about Kate?"

Rolling it over in my head a few times, I looked at him and smiled. "You know what? I think it fits her. I don't know why I didn't think of it but thank you. Now I can get her a collar and tags."

"We can grab some while we're out today. How about I go back to take Toby home and you can get ready for the day? I'll be back to pick you up in about an hour?"

"Sounds perfect. Thank you so much, Brandon."

"Don't mention it."

I watched them from the doorway as they hopped in his truck and backed out of the drive. Then it came time to shower and dress for the day.

Chapter Nine

I managed to be ready well in advance of Brandon returning, so I took the time to sit on the couch and scroll through social media. Kate snuggled in my lap, happily purring as I pet her.

By the time he knocked on the door, I had decided I needed to eat again and he found me digging through the fridge.

"First stop, food?"

Turning around and closing the fridge door, I agreed with him. "Please. For some reason, I am starving again."

"Do you want to go anywhere in particular?"

"If we plan to do some shopping why don't we just see what the restaurants at the mall have to offer? I want to get Amanda and Liam a baby gift while we are out, plus kitten stuff for Kate."

"Let's do it then."

We managed to sneak out the door without Kate trying to escape, and he held the door of the truck open for me like a gentleman. I had to admit it felt nice to be spoiled.

We managed to spend the majority of the afternoon grabbing lunch and shopping for whatever caught our fancy. I got baby gifts for the twins and everything this cat could ever possibly need in its lifetime. Stowing the purchases in the backseat, we debated what to grab for dinner.

"Why don't you call and ask Amanda what she feels like having? That way we are sure to get something she wants."

While he made the call, I used the time to get the baby gifts wrapped in tissue paper and stuck into the gift bags I had picked up, and we wound up heading to multiple places to grab food. We hit the only open fruit stand to grab stuff to make a fruit salad and then hit up the grocery store to grab steaks to grill and a couple of bottles of wine. A final stop at Francesca's got us two different dessert options, birthday cake and bite-sized cream puffs.

Francesca gushed over how quickly I had brought Brandon in to see her, and oohed and ahhed over pictures of the twins. She insisted the birthday cake was her gift to me and tucked a couple of Cassie's favorite macaroons around the edge of the box.

Thanking her with tears in my eyes, she gave me a hug and told me not to cry.

"Happy birthday darling. Enjoy!" She turned and looked at Brandon with a mock frown on her face. "And don't you take so long before you come back to see me again."

"Yes ma'am. I'll be back sooner than you might think."

We waved and headed out the door with our boxes.

"It made me happy to see her again. I can't believe I waited so long."

"That's how I felt when I came in for the first time.

Like, what had I been waiting for?"

After pulling into the driveway we managed to gather everything we needed to carry in to the house in just one trip between the two of us, but our arms were full. Brandon used the tip of his tennis shoe to knock on the door, and we could hear Liam call that he was coming from somewhere inside.

"Why didn't you just let yourselves in?" he asked as he opened the door. "Oh. That explains it."

He grabbed things for both of us to lessen our load and I followed the two of them toward the back of the house. They had a gorgeous sun room leading off to the deck and overlooking the backyard, and that's where Amanda sat snuggled up with the twins.

I sat my load on the island as she called out to me. "Jenna, happy birthday! It's so good to see you. I'm so excited you agreed to spend it with us."

I walked over and she handed up the tiny bundle wrapped in pink. "Jenna, meet Cassandra Kate."

I held her in my arms, careful to support her head as I stared into her tiny face. While I knew there would be no reason for any physical resemblance, I couldn't help but think I saw a reflection of Cassie's nature in her eyes. She stared right into my soul.

I didn't even realize I started to cry until the first droplet left my chin and created a dark spot on the satin of the blanket. I hurried to use my sleeve to mop the tears.

"Oops, I'm sorry. I didn't mean to cry on her."

Amanda giggled. "She won't melt. We bathe her all the time and she always comes out in one piece. It won't hurt her any."

I sat down next to Amanda as she introduced Cassandra's brother, Connor. Their eyes were the same color hazel and many of their features were mirror images of each other. I sat enthralled by the two tiny beings, my biological clock making its presence known yet again.

Brandon swooped in to take Connor from his mother, giving her a few moments with empty arms to relax. She smiled as she watched the two of us side by side.

"Aren't you two cute?"

His eyes met mine and we smiled. It sank in at the moment just how much I had needed companionship. I'd been dropping in on Cassie's parents at least every other week, although I tried to make it weekly, it didn't have the same effect as what I felt seeping into my soul at this moment. I'd needed this in a way that my conscious mind hadn't even been able to grasp, and I owed Brandon big time for bringing me along.

Amanda and I settled onto the sofa to talk and snuggle the babies while the men were in charge of getting dinner ready. I had offered to at least cut fruit for the salad but they were having none of my assistance. Liam even opened the wine and brought us each a glass, filling Amanda's with sparkling cider because she still nursed the twins.

The atmosphere relaxed me, the wine helped, and by the time we settled around the table to eat I felt better than I had in months and told them all so.

"I can't thank you guys enough. I didn't realize how much I missed human interaction until tonight. I appreciate you guys more than you will ever know."

Amanda reached over and touched my arm. "You are practically family to us. You're welcome any time, with or without that brute across the table," she announced, winking as she talked.

Liam nodded. "We're pretty happy to see you again

too. And what better cause than celebration for a birthday?" He raised his glass. "To Jenna, who even though she is getting older, is still the baby of the group!"

"Here here!" Brandon and Amanda echoed his sentiments as all four glasses clinked in the middle.

The noise caused one of the twins, who had been sleeping peacefully in bassinets, to fuss. I caught Amanda before she could get up.

"Please, let me."

Slipping through the doorway back into the sun room, I identified Cassandra as the noisemaker and lifted her gently into my arms.

"Shh... It's alright precious, don't cry." Cradling her close, I hummed a lullaby and swayed gently, while looking out the window into the back yard. Leaves had begun to fall and cover the grass. The sky was gray as the sun began to set, earlier and earlier now that fall had arrived. Her tiny noises ceased, and she looked up at me with wide eyes.

"You are named after one of the most amazing people to ever walk this earth. She was your auntie, and her name was Cassandra Kate too. We called her Cassie, and she was my very best friend." My voice choked up as I talked to her.

I chattered on, my voice barely above a whisper. I told her about Cassie's favorite foods and favorite color. I told her about the wedding to her uncle Brandon, and how beautiful Cassie had looked in her dress. I even told her about the birthday card from Cassie, that seemed as if had been sent from heaven.

By the time I looked back down she had returned to a peaceful sleep. I tucked her back in the bassinet and looked up to see Brandon standing in the doorway watching me.

"You're a natural with babies."

"Probably only with these two, but..." I shrugged.

"I doubt it." He gestured that I should precede him through the door. "How about some dessert?"

While I had been with the baby they had set out the desserts, put candles on the cake, and placed gifts at my seat. I was immediately teary again.

"You guys..." I held out my hands, palms up as if I couldn't find the words.

Brandon seated me and pushed my chair in, then the three of them began to sing happy birthday. Quietly, so as not to wake the tiny humans in the other room, but they sang to me nonetheless. Another small part of my heart healed in that moment.

Liam served dessert, giving me a small piece of everything. I opened the card from Amanda and Liam, then the gift, which was a beautiful scarf.

"I love it so much!" I looped the infinity circle around my neck, smiling from ear to ear.

Brandon handed over his gift. "It looks great on you."

I opened his card and smiled at his simple signature at the bottom. The purple bag held a small white box. I glanced up at him before opening the top. Nestled inside was a beautiful silver charm bracelet. He had attached three charms.

The first depicted two female silhouettes holding hands. The second looked exactly like a miniature Toby. The third one looked like a beautiful flower with my birthstone for the centerpiece. I couldn't have loved it any more. I took it out of the box and attempted to put it on.

"Do you need a little help over there?"

"Yes, please." I handed him the bracelet and held

my wrist out.

Once fastened I held up my arm to admire it, watching the light play off the charms. I threw my arms around him in an emotional hug.

"Thank you so much. I absolutely love it and the charms couldn't be more perfect!"

He wrapped his arms around me to return the hug. "There are plenty of spaces for you to add more charms too. And I'll have you know I picked everything out myself with no assistance from anyone else."

Liam whistled. "Give that boy a prize, he did good."

Amanda clapped. "Excellent job little brother. I'm so proud of you."

We all had a good laugh at his expense, waking up the babies again. I slapped my hand over my mouth and gave Amanda an apologetic look.

"Don't worry about it. It's about time for them to eat again anyways."

She settled herself in to feed them and we cleaned up the mess we had made in the kitchen and dining room. Liam made sure I had leftovers of everything to take home with me for the rest of the weekend. He handed me a paper bag with handles, full of my goodies.

"Just like take out from the best place in town, right?"

He got my happiest smile in return. "The very best place anywhere."

We said our goodbyes and got ready to leave.

"Don't be a stranger, Jenna. We love seeing you, and want to get together more often." Amanda looked to content, settled there nursing her babies.

"Thank you so much. I had the best time tonight, and I needed this more than I realized until I got it. It sure filled a part of the hole that I've been walking around with."

I leaned over and pressed my cheek against hers. She turned slightly and whispered in my ear.

"We love you."

"I love you, too."

Brandon said his goodbyes, we waved to Liam, who walked us to the door, and got into the truck. The ride back to my place found us talking very little as I sat lost in my thoughts. I'd been expecting for this birthday to be one of my worst days ever, and these people had come together and made sure it ranked as one of the best.

We pulled into my drive and Brandon turned off the engine.

"Do you want to come in for a little bit? We have more wine, and we could eat cake round two."

"Change that to coffee and you're on."

"I have coffee." We headed up the walkway and I carefully opened the door, attempting to block Kate from escaping with my foot.

She had learned her lesson though, jumping out over my foot and onto the porch. Brandon scooped her up, laughing.

"You're going to have your hands full with this one. She already knows your tricks."

"Right? Oh my goodness."

I set my bag on the dining table and went in to start coffee. Brandon grabbed the cake and split it between the two of us after grabbing plates and forks.

We settled on the couch, facing each other with plates of cake in our laps and coffee on the table next to us.

"This is the perfect end to an almost perfect birthday. Thank you so much." My bracelet clinked against the mug as I reached to pick up my coffee.

"You're welcome."

The silence between us was comfortable as we ate our cake. I pondered how things might have been different if Cassie hadn't died. Would we be out celebrating? On a trip? Maybe we would have done much the same things, just with her instead of without her.

As we finished our dessert Brandon got ready to go. I walked him to the door and thanked him again. Holding his jacket in one hand and keys in the other, he wrapped me in a hug. Resting his chin against the top of my head meant I could feel is words as well as hear them.

"You're welcome, Jenna. Thank you. You have helped keep me sane over these last few months more than you know. I don't know how I would have gotten through this without you."

"Same, Brandon. Exactly the same."

Our arms tightened briefly before releasing, and he leaned down and planted a soft kiss on my forehead.

"Happy birthday."

He walked down the front steps and gave a little

wave as he got in the truck, a smile on his face. I echoed his smile and closed the door, ready to call it a night.

Lying in bed I spent a few minutes pondering how truly blessed I was before drifting off into a restful sleep.

Chapter Ten

My first full day of being twenty-seven dawned clear and beautiful if a little chilly. Aside from throwing in a load of laundry and picking up the few dishes from our cake fest the night before, I didn't have a whole lot going on. I set the birthday cards along the coffee table to remind myself for a few days that people did, in fact, love me and I had them there if I needed support. I wanted to hang onto this feeling I had of beginning to truly heal.

Carter texted me late morning to ask if I wanted to join him for brunch.

Sure, I'm not busy. Do you want to meet somewhere or get takeout and come here?

I smiled after sending the text. Here I had yet another person who seemed to think that I might be worth their time. It helped. I'd never been particularly self-conscious, but losing Cassie had drug me down into a hole I hadn't been prepared to climb out of on my own.

I can grab coffee and breakfast and swing by if you want?

Perfect, but fair warning I am in my Sunday sweats and it would take a lot to motivate me to put real clothes on. LOL

I waited for his response, knowing that it would have a huge impact on whether or not he and I would be able to spend much time together in the future. There were some days that I just didn't feel like joining the land of the living and people in my life had to accept that. Those who didn't never lasted long.

Excellent, that means I don't have to bother to get pretty either. See you soon.

A perfect response. Too perfect? Can anyone be that perfect? Maybe. Either way, he'd said exactly the right thing for the situation and I chose to take it at face value for now. The more we got to know each other the better insight I would get into who he really was.

Deciding to at least brush my hair for the "date," I combed it out and threw it up into a bun. That met my low expectations of entertaining on the weekend. Being clean and not smelling funky made the top of the list; since I had already showered both the items could be checked off. Oh, better brush my teeth. Not that I expected there to be any kissing, but...

Less than fifteen minutes later I heard a knock at the door. Yelling that I would be right there, I looked around for Kate. She had gotten quite sneaky at trying to dash out the door, even if she as nowhere to be seen when I first headed to open it.

Her head popped up from behind a couch pillow, and I carried her to answer the door. Carter most likely had his hands full of food and not be able to catch her like Brandon had the night before.

"Well, hi there." I pulled the door wide to give him enough room to pass with his full hands, and boy were they full.

"Good morning gorgeous. How has your weekend been?"

"So far, so good, and getting better every minute."

I'd taken the liberty of deciding we would eat at the

coffee table without inquiring his preference this time, figuring we would want to be comfortable. I led him toward the living room checking to see if he wanted me to get anything from the kitchen.

"Nope, I believe we have everything we need in these brown paper bags right here."

He stopped short staring into the living room.

"Is there a problem?" He had an odd look on his face and I didn't know what to make of it.

"When was your birthday?" Ah, he'd caught sight of the cards then.

I laughed. "Yesterday. I am now the ripe old age of twenty-seven. But, shh. Don't tell anyone. It's a secret."

He didn't laugh with me. "Why didn't you tell me?"

"Um... It didn't come up?" Weird. I didn't think to mention it to him, but it's not like it was that important.

"Sure it is. I would have at least bought you a card. Got some flowers. Brought a present."

"You don't need to do that. It was a very low key affair. I spent the evening with Brandon and his sister at their place. I got to meet her new twins. They named the girl after Cassie. It was very touching."

He seemed perturbed but willing to let the subject

drop. I pushed it aside and decided to ignore it.

"I didn't know exactly what you preferred for brunch so I brought a little bit of everything."

"Boy, you aren't kidding!" Container after container appeared out of the bag. For a minute I was reminded of Mary Poppin's carpet bag that would hold everything you could ever need or want in it without getting overfull. I said so to him.

"I've never seen it."

"What?! Are you kidding me? You never saw Mary Poppin's? That movie is a classic and one of my absolute favorites. Do you want to watch it? I have it on Blu-ray. And DVD."

"Sure if you want to. You can indoctrinate me. Show me your ways, wise one." He chuckled and I laughed too.

"Coming right up."

I got the movie going and we made plates. He'd managed to get a good number of my favorite things, even without asking what they were. The perfectly cooked eggs Benedict sported fresh chives on top of the hollendaise and tasted amazing. Fried red potatoes with the perfect amount of crispiness and garlic accompanied them.

He'd included sausage and bacon, waffles, scrambled eggs and pastries as well. Drinks included coffees and the makings for mimosas.

"A girl could get used to this ya know?" I balanced my plate as I shooed Kate back down to the floor. She jumped right back onto the table as my phone vibrated across the top with a text. I grabbed it before she could chase it and make a mess, which would ruin our breakfast.

Hey day after the birthday girl. I think I might have dropped my wallet in the couch cushions last night. Could you check for me?

Yep, hold on....

I looked at Carter. "Could I bother you to stand up for just a sec?"

"Sure."

He stood, and sure enough, after a little rooting around I came up with Brandon's wallet in hand.

It's here all right.

Well, thank goodness it's not lost. Can I swing by and grab it? I won't be interrupting anything?

Carter brought me brunch, but you can still come

by.

After he agreed, I forewarned Carter.

"Brandon needs to stop by and pick up his wallet. He must have dropped it last night."

"Oh? I thought you guys were at his sister's?"

"We came back here to polish off the cake and wine. Well, I had wine. He had coffee since he had to drive home. If people keep feeding me I'm going to have to join a gym or something."

Carter looked at me, one corner of his mouth turned down in a semi-frown. "Are you sure I'm not getting between something? I feel a little odd about this."

"Not at all. He was married to my very best friend. We've leaned on each other a lot to get through her loss, but it doesn't go any farther than that."

"Okay." He drew out the word slightly, as if not quite believing me but not doubting me enough to call me out on it.

I began hoping he wasn't the jealous type. Brandon and I became close after losing Cassie and I wouldn't be persuaded to end that friendship for any new relationship.

We heard a knock and the front door open. I heard

Toby coming before I saw him.

"Easy Toby!"

He came bounding into the living room, excited to see me but stopped short when he saw Carter. He stood next to me and growled slightly.

"Toby, no. Be nice. He's okay."

Brandon entered the room. "Sorry about that. I should have known he'd be too excited to walk in here calmly."

I stood. "That's okay. He knows he's home here too. Brandon this is Carter, Carter, Brandon."

The two exchanged pleasantries and shook hands. I couldn't help but compare the two a little since they stood side by side.

Carter wasn't short by any means, but Brandon had a good five or six inches on him. Brandon had dark hair and amber eyes, where Carter had blue eyes and light brown hair. Seemingly polar opposites at first glance.

I handed Brandon his wallet. "Here ya go. What are you two up to today?"

"Taking Toby to the dog park for a romp and then running a few errands in town. Nothing exciting. You?"

"Brunch, obviously," I said waving my hand

towards the food, "then I haven't decided yet."

"Have a good day. Call me if you need anything."
He turned to Carter. "Nice to meet you."

Carter just nodded, which I found rather rude, and
raised his hand in a wave.

"I'll walk you to the front door. Come on Toby.
Time to go bye-bye."

But Toby had decided Kate made far too interesting
of game, hiding under the coffee table frame just out of
reach. He whined, pleasing her to come out and play
with him and she just hissed in response.

"Come on boy, she doesn't want to play with you.
The next time you spend the night you two can get to
know each other."

Brandon came over and grabbed his collar. Toby
sighed and gave up, agreeing to follow Brandon out the
door. I didn't worry much about Kate trying to escape
this time, seeing as how Toby stood between her and the
great outdoors.

I gave Toby loves and a biscuit from the canister in
the front hall, sending the two on their way with a wave.
My return to the living room found Carter staring at the
paused television.

"He was married to your friend?"

"Yep. He had planned to propose to Cassie during a dinner cruise on their vacation in Hawaii, but she had a snorkeling accident and almost drowned that day. So they spent it in the hospital instead and he saved it for another time. When they got home Cassie found out she had the tumor almost immediately. He proposed the minute she told him about but she said no, thinking he had only done it out of pity. He pestered her some more and she finally said yes."

I smiled at the memory of their wedding. Cassie had looked radiant that day, in spite of all the weight she had lost and the bags under her eyes. She was every inch the blushing bride.

"They had a gorgeous wedding in her backyard and their honeymoon to Barcelona was the last trip she was able to take." My smile faltered a little at that.

"I'm sorry, I didn't mean to make you sad by asking about her."

"No, no. Not at all. I mean, yes it still makes me sad, but I love to talk about her. I could spend all day telling you about her and never get tired of it."

"Okay then. Tell me more about her. I learn a lot

about you that way too."

I took a deep breath, appreciating fully that he willingly sat to listen to me gush about someone I had lost just to learn about me and make me feel better.

"You asked for it!"

I told him many of my favorite memories, beginning with how we met. I jumped around from story to story, ending with the trip we took to Vegas right after she got her diagnosis.

"She was already tired so much of the time, but we had a blast. I got a suite at the Cosmopolitan and we did all the fun things that you are supposed to do on a girls trip to Las Vegas. We saw shows, ate good food, had a few drinks... Those memories are priceless to me now. The pictures we took are some of my favorites ever, and I have big plans to get them printed and framed to hang on the walls here soon."

"She sounds like she was an amazing person. How come you haven't framed them yet?"

"Honestly? After she died I fell into a pretty deep hole. The party for Dana where we first met? That was the first time I had gone out since her memorial service. I didn't see anyone outside of my own family but her parents and Brandon for weeks. A couple of months actually."

"Wow. I'm so sorry you lost her. I can't imagine how hard it must be. I haven't lost anyone close to me yet, but I dread the day because I know that eventually, it will happen."

"It sucks. Big time. But it's one of those things that you can't control, so you just try and cope as best you can. I've just been getting myself back these last couple weeks. And you've helped me with that, so thank you."

His surprise showed on his face. "Wow. Thanks for giving me your number then, and letting me be a part of your healing. I would have had no idea."

I smiled at him. "You don't need to thank me, I'm pretty glad I gave you my number."

Chapter Eleven

The weeks following my birthday both dragged on interminably slow and sped by too fast for comfort. Before I knew it the calendar showed only a single week until Cassie's birthday. Thanksgiving had come and gone, and we weathered our first one without her as best we could. Early December had brought a mild winter so far, but that particular day dawned blustery and cold.

Carter and I had been seeing each other off and on. He seemed vaguely uncomfortable with the amount of time I spent with Brandon though, and I couldn't quite pin down how I was supposed to deal with that. Brandon and I got together at least once a week, and I frequently visited his sister and the twins.

I loaded the car with what I had offered to bring for brunch that day and got ready to head over to Cassie's house. I still called it her house, even though Brandon was the only one that lived there. It would probably always be her house to me, even if he ended up selling it someday. If he ever did maybe I would buy it for myself, but even then I would be living in Cassie's house. Some things will never change.

Before I got the car in reverse my phone dinged with a text message. Carter wanted to know if I had any plans. I sighed, unsure if I should tell him I did and they happened to be with Brandon. I'd already told him we got together regularly.

I decided to keep it simple and tell him yes, but that I would be free later on in the afternoon. He took so long to respond that I had given up and started driving by the time he texted back. Safety first, now he had to wait until I got there for an answer.

His reply said that he would be busy in the afternoon but would call me late evening. That worked for me and I told him so, putting my phone in my purse to head in the house.

Brandon greeted me at the door, opening it for me. Toby made an excellent doorbell and I never had to wait to be let in. We went back to the dining room and I set my bags on the island.

"How are you holding up? I feel like it's been a really long week." He looked a little haggard and I worried about him.

"Aside from sleeping like shit, I guess I'm doing okay. These next few weeks have repeated special days so close together, and I'm afraid I will backslide. Which is weird because I've been doing really well."

"I hear you. I realized that I am more worried about how I will spend her birthday than I ever was about how I would spend mine. Then it's something every couple of weeks."

Brandon named them off, holding up a finger for each one as he talked. "Her birthday. Christmas. New Year's Eve. Then my birthday. Then Valentine's Day. Then we find ourselves back in April. Our anniversary and the first anniversary of her death." He sighed.

"I think if we can make it through this first year, all

the following ones will be a little bit easier. Do you want to get together to celebrate her birthday, or would you rather be alone?"

He shook his head. "I don't know. I want to say that I would rather be alone, but I don't know if that would be the healthiest thing for me."

We moved fluidly together, getting breakfast ready and sitting down at the table with our coffees. Before we had a chance to start eating Toby began to bark, running for the front door.

"Expecting anyone?"

"Not that I know of." Brandon stood and headed to the front door while I sipped my coffee. I heard low voices murmuring, and he took a few minutes before returning with a medium-sized shipping box in his hands.

"You got a present?"

"That was Cassie's lawyer. Apparently she set up something else for us." He turned the box so that I could see her familiar writing on the front, with instructions to "please open with Jenna."

"She sure made a lot of assumptions that we'd still be talking to one another at this point."

He smiled. "She probably figured she could will it from heaven no matter what the two of us thought we had decided for ourselves."

"I don't doubt that for a minute."

The conversation came to a stop as we both stared at the box, uncertain if we were ready to open it and see what she had left us inside. Brandon retrieved a knife from the block, laying it on the top of the box. He pushed it my way.

"Do you want to open it?"

"I'll do it if you want me to."

He just nodded. I slit the packing tape carefully, unsure if whatever was inside might be vulnerable to the blade. A brightly colored file folder lay on top. I pulled it out and set it on the table. Underneath it sat two flat boxes, tied with purple ribbon. I laid those out as well.

"File folder first, I guess?"

He gave me another nod.

Opening it up, I found a type written note from the lawyer lying flat on top. I read it aloud to him. Cassie had apparently given her very specific instructions as to what she wanted him to do for her, down to providing him with the packages that she wanted him to put in the box. He ended it with his signature and the instructions to call him if we had any questions.

"What is she up to now?" I couldn't help but be touched that she had gone to all this trouble for us, knowing she would not be here.

Moving the type-written sheet exposed lined notebook paper folded in half. I opened it to reveal Cassie's handwriting.

Hi you guys! It's almost time for happy birthday to me. And I wanted to be absolutely certain the two of you spent my birthday actually being happy. So I planned a little surprise for you. In this folder, you will find an itinerary, some plane tickets, some show tickets and a couple presents. I booked you guys a trip to Vegas!! Woohoo, you guys are going to have so much fun. I booked you guys the same suite we stayed at when Jenna and I went to Vegas last time, the view is fantastic. (Don't worry, it has two beds. But even if it didn't those beds are huge and you could fit ten people in there.) Look it over and go pack. You leave in five days. I love both of you and I want you to enjoys yourselves. The entire trip is on me, by me, for me. Go celebrate me like I would celebrate either one of you.

Lots of love, Cassie

I looked up, meeting Brandon's eyes. "She booked us a trip? To Vegas. Together." I laughed out loud. "She is bossier in death than she ever was alive."

He just shook his head, lips half quirked up in a smile but his eyebrows drawn together in thought.

"We don't have to go if you don't want to. I can stay here and you can go, or-"

"Jenna stop. I'd love to go. I think we will have a lot of fun. I'm just surprised that she did all this."

"I shouldn't be, but so am I. Talk about out of the blue. She must have begun planning as soon as she knew."

I opened the envelope. It was the itinerary. "She has us flying out Friday morning and coming back on Monday. Is that okay with you?"

"Yep, works out fine."

Putting that aside I grabbed the next envelope and held it out to him. "Your turn."

He opened it slowly. "Tickets to Cirque du Soleil for Friday night. 'O' at the Bellagio."

"Ooh fancy. We saw Ka at the MGM when we went and it was incredible."

The other envelopes held one more set of show tickets and some admissions to the more popular attractions on the strip. The final one held the information on the limo company that she had booked for our round trip from the airport to the hotel and back again. Next were the two little boxes. Each had one of our names on the top, although they looked to be the exact same other than that. I handed Brandon his.

"Open on three? One, two, three..."

We both lifted the lids to our box. A small not rested on top.

I told you the whole trip was on me. Go wild, have fun, spend money like you don't have a care in the world. Gamble, shop, whatever. Buy yourself a birthday gift on my behalf. Think of me while you do all the fun things! I love you.

Underneath the note lay a stack of hundred dollar bills. I looked at Brandon, shocked. This little box held a lot of money. He picked up his stack and counted it. In the end, each of us had five thousand dollars.

"Oh. My. God. We can't spend this much money in four days! And she knows I don't gamble."

Brandon laughed out loud. A deep belly laugh that I

had not heard from him in a long time. "Girl, if there is one thing you women can do, is spend money."

His continued laughter got me going to, and I could barely breathe let alone talk.

"This is still a shit-ton of money for just a few days."

He met my eyes and winked. "We'll make a good faith effort, okay? If we have any left over we'll promise to take another trip and spend it there. Deal?"

I rolled the thought over in my head for a second. "You've got a deal."

I took the note she had written and slipped it in my purse so I could have it close to me whenever I wanted to pull it out and look at it.

"It's a good thing I'm traveling with a big strong guy like you. I'd be afraid to carry that kind of cash on my otherwise!"

"Don't worry, I will protect you and your wallet."

We laughed, reheated our food and finished our brunch. I gathered up my stuff to head home once we had decided on the details of getting to the airport from home. (He offered to drive.)

He walked me to the front door, Toby dancing

alongside us. "Well, I guess I will see you Friday morning then?"

"I'm looking forward to it." Kissing Toby and waving to Brandon, I headed out the door.

On the way home I realized I did not look forward to telling Carter about the trip. While we weren't exactly what I'd call serious, we had been dating a couple of months now and we had both agreed that neither of us would be seeing other people.

Not that this was a date. It was Brandon, for crying out loud. But I didn't know if he would see it that way. He still seemed to have reservations about the time I spent with Brandon, not that he had actually said anything to me. But his reactions were obvious a lot of the time when I talked about him or mentioned something we had done.

We made plans via text for him to come by once he finished whatever plans he had for the afternoon and he offered to bring dinner. I figured I could tell him then.

He arrived with burgers and fries, looking worn out.

"Long afternoon? You look tired."

"Yeah, I helped a buddy tear down an old wood shed and put up the new one, then moved all the wood into the new one."

"Yikes, sounds like a lot of work."

We ate in front of the television and chatted, the way we did many nights that we spent in. Before I could bring up the trip, he asked if I had plans for the next weekend.

"I do actually. Cassie surprised me with a trip to Vegas for Brandon and I to celebrate her birthday. She paid for everything and had the tickets and information delivered to us this morning by her lawyer."

"What? Like she planned it all before she died?"

"Yes. She gave her lawyer explicit instructions. The plane tickets are booked, she bought show tickets and booked the hotel and everything."

"You guys are sharing a hotel room?" I could hear Carter's jealousy raising its ugly head.

"Yes, but there are two beds, don't worry."

"I don't know if I like this Jenna. It seems odd to me that you claim there isn't anything between the two of you and yet you are sharing a hotel room on a trip to Vegas together. That's the kind of things couples do."

"Carter. There is nothing. We are friends. That's all."

"Would you like it if the shoe was on the other foot and it was me jetting off to Vegas for a weekend with another girl?"

I sighed. "If the situation was exactly the same, I would understand."

He stood up. "I need to get going. I'll call you later this week, okay?"

"Carter please don't leave mad."

"I'm not mad, Jenna." He held up his hand as I started to stand. "I can see myself out."

I looked after him, dumbfounded. "Don't let the cat out," I called down the hallway.

The only response was the door closing solidly behind him.

"Kate. Here kitty kitty." I called for her, even though I knew he would never let her get out and then just shut the door.

She looked up from her pillow on the couch, unconcerned with my desire to talk things out with her.

"Men can be such idiots."

She looked at me in the disdainful way cats do, meowed and went back to sleep.

"Some gal pal you are."

Chapter Twelve

The week sped by. Each day I found myself looking forward to the trip just a little bit more. My last trip to Vegas had been full of good memories made, and I looked forward to a positive experience.

I checked the weather app a hundred times as I tried to decide what to pack. In the end, I only tossed in a few favorites to get me through and decided to shop for anything else I needed. Adding is a makeup and toiletry bag I called it good and zipped it shut, sitting in the hall by the front door. That was Tuesday.

Thursday I hauled it back to my room again to take inventory and be extra sure I had all the things I wanted. Aside from adding an extra pair of shoes, nothing changed and I laughed out loud at myself as I rolled back down the hall to takes its place by the front door once more.

We had planned for Brandon to come by and pick me up at eight Friday morning and we would leave his car in airport parking. I had gotten a second litter box for Kate and set up two stations with those automatic feeders and water dishes. She had a new cat condo and a zillion toys to keep her busy while I went on my trip.

According to popular opinion, cats are notoriously self-sufficient and I didn't need to worry about her while I was away. Unable to accept that such a young kitten would be fine all by itself for four days, I had asked my sister to come by daily and spend some time with her. She would be staying over with Toby and taking care of him while we were gone also.

The night before we caught the plane I lay in bed thinking about the last time Cassie and I had gone. We had crammed so much into those few days, even with her exhaustion. We'd go until she felt too tired to go anymore, and then return to the room so she could rest. Once she felt better we were running around town again.

I felt bad she had booked such an expensive suite since we would probably barely spend any time in it, but oh well. I appreciated her even more, knowing she had planned all this with the knowledge that she wouldn't be here to enjoy it. Until the very end, she had used her time and energy to think of us.

Friday morning, I found myself wide awake at 5:00 am, in spite of the fact that my alarm had been set for 8:00. Too excited to go back to sleep I got up and got ready for the day.

Brandon must have had trouble sleeping too because he texted me at six to see if I wanted to leave early and grab breakfast.

Yes, please! I have been up since 5 and I'm just waiting for the time to pass.

On my way.

He must have been ready to walk out the door because less than fifteen minutes later he pulled into the drive and walked up the front steps.

"Couldn't sleep?"

I shook my head. "Not at all."

"Me either." He grinned and held his hand out for my suitcase. "Where do you want to have breakfast?"

"I don't care. We could get to the airport early and eat there? Then we wouldn't have to worry about timing and whether or not the line to get through security is ten miles long or not."

"Excellent idea. Wanna stop for a coffee on the way?"

"Um, yeah. When do I not want to stop for coffee?"

More laughter and he backed out of the driveway headed for our favorite coffee stand. Coffee procured, we proceeded to battle a little bit of the morning rush hour traffic on the way to the airport but got there in plenty of time to check out bags and have a leisurely breakfast. We wandered the few airport shops and still made it to our gate with a half an hour til we needed to board.

"You know, when Cassie and I came I'm pretty sure we were at the gate right across from where we are now."

"She had so much fun on that trip. She talked about so much, and we must have looked through the pictures a hundred time. I'm so glad you guys made it down."

"It was amazing. I think the amount of fun I had on that trip is what led to me be so excited about this one. That, and being thankful for how much she planned in advance to be sure we had a good time..." I trailed off, feeling a slight pang of guilt.

She should be the one flying to Vegas with her husband, not me. I got angry at how unfair life treated some people while others had all the time in the world.

I startled as Brandon touched my leg gently. "She wouldn't want you to be sad, and you know it."

"Am I that obvious? I just had a thought that it's unfair that you and I are doing this instead of you and her. She deserved all the good things life had to offer."

"She did. But I had an epiphany a while back that changed the way I see it. I sit out on the porch swing some nights, just watching the stars, and it came to me out of nowhere."

I looked over and met his eyes, curious. "Yeah?"

"She deserved so much, I realized that in order for her to get all things she deserved, she couldn't get them here on Earth. She was better than that. We hurt because we look at it through the filter of seeing all she has lost and missed out on, but what if we turn it around? Think of all the things she has gained. Neither of us were ever particularly religious, but heaven has got to be an awesome place. I think maybe she is up there reveling in all that glory, waiting until our turn to join her comes along."

I stared at him speechless for a minute. He had rendered me actually speechless. I'd been so mired down in my own pain, that I hadn't ever thought to look at it from another direction.

"You know," I began quietly, "that is the most peaceful statement I have ever heard. As in, it brings me peace. My heart still hurts for us, because we lost something so beautiful, but you are ultimately right. She is somewhere far better."

A single tear escaped and he reached over and wiped it away, then handed me the napkin that he'd wrapped around his coffee cup.

"Don't cry."

"That tear came from joy. I promise." I grinned. "I think you just changed something amazing for me. Thank you."

We sat in silence for a few minutes watching the throngs of people rushing to wherever they needed to be.

Families ushering tiny children while simultaneously juggling diaper bags and suitcases. Older folks strolling along to their gate. Young people, laughing boisterously.

"You know, she first told me the news on that porch swing. I thought it had to be some sort of sick joke, even though that had never been her style. She looked over my way and started to laugh, asking me if she *looked* like she was dying." I shook my head. "We started her bucket list that night, and Vegas was on it."

"She told me about it. She said you were the very first person she told because she knew that no matter what you would be there for her until the very end."

Before I could respond they began boarding announcements for our flight. In true Cassie style, we were booked in first class and among the first to board. Because we had checked out bags all I had to worry about was my purse and jacket. Brandon guided me toward the line and I shook off the melancholy, my excitement growing again.

After a short flight, we touched down to a sunny, beautiful day. The limo met us bearing a placard with Brandon's last name and whisked us to the hotel. Cassie had thought of everything and we received special attention, being led through VIP check-in and the bellhop taking our bags up to our room.

"Boy she must have bribed them with a ton of cash." Brandon's wry smile gave away how much he enjoyed it in spite of the sardonic statement.

"That's just like her though. Now I feel like we should be watching around every corner because we have no idea what else she had up her sleeve when she did all this!"

The suite was beautiful, just like last time, and a complimentary bottle of champagne sat chilling on the table.

I pulled it out of the bucket and held it up. "It's five o'clock somewhere, right?"

Taking it from me he began uncorking it. "It's never too early in Vegas."

He poured us both a generous glass and we took it out to the patio. Sitting in the comfortable chairs we watched the Bellagio fountains go off and relaxed.

Back inside we pulled out all the tickets she had purchased ahead of time, laying out the ones that were for certain days and times in their chronological order. Friday night we had Cirque du Soleil for the seven o'clock show.

"Should we freshen up, grab dinner and walk down for the show?" Brandon looked over the other items as he spoke.

"We can do that. Want me to tuck the tickets to the other places in my purse, so we have them with us if we decide to do one of them?"

"That's a good idea. Where do you want to eat?"

"Well, the buffet at the Bellagio is amazing..."

"Sold! Let's get ready to go."

I changed in the bathroom since I had more clothes to swap out while he got ready in the bedroom area. Fifteen minutes later both of us were ready to walk out the door.

"You look very nice," he complimented me.

"Thanks, you do too. Are you hungry?"

"Starved. Let's go."

Double-checking to be sure we had the room keys we headed out. We took our time since we still had a couple hours before the show and admired the sights along the way. The two hotels are close together, and we stopped to catch the fountains again from street level before making our way to the buffet.

Dinner tasted delicious and both of us ate way more than we should have, but declared the discomfort worth it, laughing as we made our way toward the theater. We posed for souvenir photos before heading inside. Our tickets were VIP, as were our seats, and we had popcorn and mixed drink slushies to enjoy during the show.

We sat speechless through the entire performance except for a few oohs and ahhs, and clapping. On the way out we stopped to see our photos and purchased every single one. Why not? She had given us the money to spend and the pictures made good memories.

The rest of our first night we spent wandering the strip and shopping. I bought a ton of clothes at Ross and laughed as he stared at the number of bags I had, compared to his single one.

"It's a good thing we made that our last stop for the night, because either way all that stuff needs to be taken back to the room. You're going to need to buy another suitcase to get all that back home."

"Probably," I giggled, "but Ross sells those too."

Shaking his head, he steered me the correct way to the elevator. Maybe I'd had a drink or two more than I needed for the evening.

Back in the room, I dropped my bags on the table, taking my pajamas into the bathroom to change. By the time I got back out, he was laying on the far bed.

"You don't have a bed preference do you?"

"Nope. They both sleep the same to me."

The two of us lay there quietly for a few minutes before I spoke up.

"Hey Brandon?"

"Yeah?"

"I had an amazing day today. Thank you."

"Me too, Jen. Me too." He reached over and shut off the lamp. "Good night."

"Night."

Chapter Thirteen

The smell of coffee roused me from my sleep, and I looked over to see a cup on the nightstand next to me. I could see the room darkening curtains cracked and assumed Brandon sat on the patio enjoying his coffee. Before even getting out of bed to start the day I took a drink.

"Mmm... that is so good."

I say my reflection in the mirror across the room and snorted at myself. Hair sticking up every which way and Not even out from under the covers, but I had my coffee.

"Good, huh?" Brandon called from the patio.

"So good. Thank you so much!"

I got out of bed, mostly because I had to pee, and then joined him on the patio. We got another sunny day, if quite chilly that early in the morning.

"What's on the agenda for today boss?"

"Hang on and I'll grab the tickets out of my purse and we can make a game plan." I got the envelope and settled in my deck chair with my coffee.

"Let's see. Shark Reef, Siegfried and Roy's Magical Garden, Titanic and the Bodies Exhibitions, and a trip to the top of the Eiffel Tower at Paris."

"They all sound like fun. What do you want to do first?"

"Well, Shark Reef is at Mandalay Bay and the Titanic and Bodies Exhibitions are at Luxor. They're right next door to each other. So why don't we grab an easy breakfast, head on over to the Shark Reef, then we can work our way back to the other two and when we're finished we can find somewhere for lunch? Sound good?"

"You're the planner for the day so I shall follow

wherever you lead. As you can see, I've already showered – sleepyhead – so I'll wait out here while you get ready."

"Okay, give me fifteen or twenty minutes. That should be plenty."

I dug through my new clothes and picked out a cute jumpsuit and grabbed the other necessities out of my suitcase. I showered in record speed and twisted my wet hair up into a bun. A little mascara, a little bit of lip gloss and I declared myself ready to face the world.

"I'm ready when you are," I called out to the balcony.

The morning flew by, and we had a fantastic time everywhere we went. We took a ton of pictures at the aquarium and stopped to look at anything that caught our interest.

The Bodies Exhibit grossed him out, and it downright amazed me. I felt like a little kid in a candy store who just wanted to touch everything so badly but knew I couldn't because the signs said so, which meant all I could do was get real close and try to commit them to memory since photos weren't allowed either.

The Titanic display left both of us in awe. Looking

at the actual items they had managed to salvage from the ship itself and imagining the people who had owned them made me feel humbled. My heart broke for the fear they must have felt on that cold, dark night. Touching the iceberg gave me the shivers; I couldn't imagine my entire body floating in water that cold.

They gave you little cards at the beginning of the walk through with a real passenger's information on it and at the end, you get to see if you survived or not. Both of us died.

"Well, I guess a cruise is out." I shrugged. Boats far from land didn't seem like the best use of my time anyways.

We browsed the souvenir shop, collected our photos (which we had done at every opportunity so far) and I bought a little teacup and saucer that exactly matched the ones they had used on the ship. I needed to buy a backpack instead of carrying a purse so I'd have something to put all my purchases in and not have to carry the bags.

"So, are you ready for lunch?" Brandon grabbed my bag and carried it for me.

"I'm getting hungry, but we've done a ton of

walking and what I am really ready for is some time to sit down!"

"That sounds good. Where do you want to eat?"

"Well we can hit the food court or buffet here, or anything between here and our room. The buffet at the hotel is supposed to be really good."

"Let's do the one at the hotel. We can run upstairs first and drop our stuff off so we don't have to lug it around while we eat."

Just as we reached our room my phone rang. Carter. I held it up and asked Brandon to wait.

"Give me just a minute?"

"Of course." He stepped out to the balcony.

"Hello?"

"Hey Jenna. What are you doing? Wanna meet up for lunch?"

I sighed. "Carter, I told you I'd be out of town all weekend. We can get together Tuesday after I get back though. Dinner?"

"You actually went? Spending a weekend out of town with another man even though I told you it bothered me?"

"Please don't start this."

"Start what? I told you it made me uncomfortable and you did it anyways. That's disrespectful."

"You know what, I'm not going to do this now. I want to enjoy my vacation. I'll be happy to talk about it with you when I get home. I can call you Monday night or we can catch up on Tuesday."

"Don't bother."

"What's that supposed to mean?" I got nothing but silence in response. "Carter? Carter? That childish jerk just hung up on me," I fumed at the ploy.

Brandon came back in from outside. "Problems?"

"Ugh. He's jealous. He didn't want me to come on the trip to begin with and I did it anyways so now he's acting all butt-hurt about it."

"Why didn't he want you to come?"

I rubbed my forehead, hoping to rub away the tension headache that I felt forming. "He's just jealous. He says I spend way too much time with you and that spending the weekend in a hotel room with another man is wrong."

Brandon laughed out loud. "Really? Sounds like maybe he's a little too insecure for his own good."

"Whatever it is I'm not dealing with it. We've only

been dating a couple of months and he doesn't own me."

"Good for you."

"Let's go eat. I'm starving now."

We ambled down to the hotel buffet, getting caught up in the lunch rush and we had to wait in line for forty-five minutes.

"It had better be good!" Brandon exclaimed as his stomach growled loudly.

I laughed at him, as did the couple in front of us in line.

The man turned around. "It's fantastic, which is why the line is so long. If you come again when it's not peak meal times you can usually get in within a few minutes."

"That's good to know, thanks." I smiled at him as the woman turned around.

We introduced ourselves.

"I'm Jenna, and this is Brandon."

"Nice to meet you. I'm Jason and this is my wife Serena. Are you guys here for anything in particular?"

I didn't look at Brandon as I answered. "We came in remembrance of a friend. Her birthday would have been tomorrow, and this is the first one without her."

"I'm so sorry for your loss. But what a fantastic way to honor her memory." Serena looked briefly sad at the mention of loss but covered it up quickly.

"Thank you. She actually planned this for us and set everything up ahead of time."

"Wow!" Jason was impressed. "She must have been a fantastic friend."

"Oh, she was. That she was."

Brandon stood quietly as we chatted. Before long it was their turn to be seated.

"Perhaps we'll run into one another again. Enjoy your lunch!"

Brandon waved and smiled, "Thanks, you too."

We got our table a couple of minutes after and wandered the buffet line quietly. We both grabbed a little bit of everything on our first trip through.

When we sat down at the table again I looked at Brandon. "I'm sorry if bringing her up made you uncomfortable."

"No, that's not it at all. I just had a minute where I really missed her."

We both ate too much and had our phones out Googling what else we wanted to do for the rest of the day. We planned to save the Eiffel Tower visit for her birthday the next night. Since we had a second show that evening we decided to just wander the strip and take in the sights until we needed to go back and get ready.

We walked for miles, all the way down one side of the strip and the back up the other. We stopped into most of the hotels to check out the decor and the shops. In spite of having had too much lunch we bought gelato in Caesar's Palace and both got the tall slushy drinks from Fat Tuesday.

We discovered Carlo's Bakery and ordered more sweets after standing at the window to watch them make the baked goods.

"Wanna take a gondola ride?" Brandon stood looking down at them as they glided across the clear blue waterway.

"Sure, why not? They look like fun."

We got our tickets and got in line, watching the couples and families ahead of us. As we got in they had us pose for souvenir photos (because every place in Vegas seemed to make money that way) and we laughed when the operator wanted us to kiss.

"No, no. Thank you, this is fine." We had scooted

close together and Brandon threw his arm around my shoulders.

The camera flashed and we got the ticket to use at the pickup area when we finished our ride. The gondolier sang to us as we followed the lazy river of water under the bridge, then into the hotel itself and back out again. It was a fun trip, and something I had not done before.

We made our way to the photo stand at the end and looked at the pictures. I knew I'd be buying them anyway, but we still discussed whether we "needed" more photos.

The lady running it commented. "You two make such a lovely couple! Why wouldn't you want all the reminders of your trip together? Are you here for a special occasion? An anniversary, maybe?"

"Oh, we uh..." Brandon stuttered.

I cut in. "We're just friends. But I do like to collect the photos. We'll take them, thank you."

She looked taken aback for a moment but rang us up, completing the rest of our transaction in silence until we walked away.

"Have a nice day."

I waved at her. "We will, thank you. You too."

"Well, that was awkward."

Looking up at Brandon I thought I caught him blushing a little. "I'm sorry, I didn't mean to lose my composure."

"Don't worry about it. It's not like I'm offended," I reassured him. "Besides, you're young. Eventually, you will have someone else in your life. She wanted that for you. She told me so, and I know she told you too."

He ran his hand over his face, not answering me right away. "I know she did. She worried about it so much I think she would have lined up my next girlfriend before she passed away if she could have." He gave a little bark of laughter. "I'm surprised she didn't hand out applications for me to go over."

"Well, we don't know that she didn't. Maybe she set them up to only come meet you after a certain amount of time."

I started to giggle, imagining Brandon waking up one day to a line of ladies outside the house, all holding applications that Cassie had personally given her stamp of approval. He glanced sideways at me, making me laugh even harder.

Once I had my giggles under control I verbalized the picture in my head, and he stared at me with a horrified look on his face.

"She would never."

That got me laughing again. "You're right she'd probably send them by one at a time so as not to overwhelm you!"

"Okay, no more alcohol for you. It's time we got you back to the room and in bed." His expression didn't give away whether he was teasing or serious, but probably a bit of both.

"Then it's a good thing we are so close to the hotel." I giggled. "Can we stop and grab something to eat? I'm getting hungry."

In spite of having eaten junk food off and on since lunch, I started to feel like I could use some real food, which would help soak up some of this alcohol too.

"Of course. You wanna grab something or order room service when we get back upstairs?"

"Let's take a look at the room service menu. Real food sounds better than fast food right now."

"I agree."

We perused the menu and Brandon called to order

while I took a quick shower, hoping to sober up a little, and got my pajamas on. My timing was perfect; I heard the knock at the door announcing our food had arrived just as I exited the bathroom.

"I'll get it," I called to Brandon who had moved out to the patio.

I opened the door and they rolled the cart in, covered in far more stuff than I remembered asking for.

I thanked the guy and tipped him just as Brandon came in the door.

"Did you get hungry while you ordered?"

He laughed. "I couldn't decide what I wanted. We have a fridge, whatever doesn't get eaten we can save for later."

Taking our plates to the table we sat and enjoyed our meal. The food was good, and we chatted about the day before climbing into bed.

Laying there in the dark, I thought about Cassie, and how we ended up here because of her. Tomorrow we would celebrate her life in a way we might not have gotten to otherwise. I had a feeling it would be a bittersweet day.

Chapter Fourteen

I woke in our hotel suite long before the sun came up that Sunday morning. Normally Cassie and I would sleep in, have coffee, and then move on to our plans for the day. The scenario I found myself in instead seemed surreal.

Brandon still slept in the bed across from me. We had the room darkening curtains pulled tightly shut, so I couldn't see a thing, but I could hear his deep breathing in the silence. He lay virtually motionless, and I worried about how he would handle today. So far he seemed to be healing quite well, having been a widower for seven months at that point.

I knew that I, too, had begun to heal. When she came to mind now I cried less and smiled more. Thinking of the effort she had gone to just to make sure Brandon and I took this trip and had the best time possible, I almost laughed out loud. My mind's eye could clearly picture her sitting in her lawyer's office with a checklist, leaving him detailed instructions of every last detail she wanted carried out.

And the patient man must have agreed to do it all. Surely she had paid him well, but I didn't know how many attorneys felt their time might not be better spent on tasks other than delivering birthday cards and planning trips to Las Vegas.

In spite of the chill, I took my comforter from the bed and went out onto the veranda to watch the sun come up. As it peeked over the horizon for the first time the sun brought gorgeous streaks of color across the sky. I watched them change hue and morph into different shades of brilliance as the sun climbed.

Brandon made his way outside just as the colors were starting to fade.

"Good morning. You missed a beautiful sunrise."

"And you didn't wake me up to see it? What kind of crap is that? How could you let me miss out?" He teased me, his laughter crinkling the corners of his eyes.

"I doubt you would have wanted me to wake you when I woke up. I had to lay there for an hour and a half before the sun even started to come up."

"Couldn't sleep?"

"Actually I slept like a baby. But when I woke up that was it. I couldn't go back to sleep. And I tried. But that's okay, this made it all worth it."

"I made coffee and it should be ready by now. Want a cup?"

"Oh yes please. You are the best." I stood up to drag my blanket back to my bed.

"I can bring it to you if you want?" he offered.

"Thanks, but I am ready to come in. It's still chilly, and I want to warm up."

Perched in our respective beds we discussed what we wanted to do for our final day in Vegas. Just as we decided to get ready to go out and find some breakfast a knock sounded at the door?

Our eyes met, and we both shrugged.

"Room service!"

"Did you order?"

He shook his head and went to answer the door. The hotel staff brought in two rolling carts, their tops full of dishes. When they had the carts situated they pulled an envelope from the lower shelf and handed it to Brandon, as I watched in surprise from my spot on the bed.

They also pulled out a white bakery box with a bow on top, and that's when I knew for sure this was part of our trip that Cassie must have arranged beforehand. She was a sneaky one, my best friend.

After they had made sure we didn't need anything else they left and left us staring at each other with wide eyes. I glanced toward the envelope in Brandon's hand, curious.

He held it out. "Do you want to open it?"

I started to shake my head. "What if it's for you?"

"Nope. It has both our names on the front." He turned it around so I could see, and sure enough, our names were scrawled in Cassie's very recognizable penmanship.

"You do it." My voice came out as a whisper, although I couldn't say why. It's not like I had anything to be afraid of.

"Okay."

He ripped the envelope open careful not to tear it and pulled out a single sheet of notebook paper. He read it to himself at first, and I had to remind him to speak out loud.

"I want to hear too!"

He shook his head, a blush staining his cheeks, and handed me the paper. What on Earth had she written in there?

Hey you two! Good morning. Happy Birthday to me! I ordered you breakfast. I hope it wasn't too early and I hope they didn't interrupt anything (wink, wink).

I jerked my eyes away from the paper and looked up at Brandon. He had found the city skyline captivating all of a sudden and didn't look at me, so I turned my attention back to the note.

Knowing the two of you I'm sure they didn't, but maybe they should have. When in Vegas, right? Okay, you know I'm just giving you a hard time. But just know that if the two of you ever decide to give it a go, nobody would be happier than me. What would be better than the two people I love most in the world finding love with each other? Don't laugh at me. I'm serious. I won't push it, obviously, but maybe my nudge in the right direction will plant the seed in the back of your minds. Anyways, I hope you guys are having a fabulous time and enjoying the shit out of Vegas. Eat, drink and be merry. I want you to spend this day celebrating me with happy thoughts and happy adventures. Live it up! Know that I would be doing the same thing for you if our places were reversed. I love you both. XOXOXO Cassie

"Oh for crying out loud," I muttered.

"Look, don't be offended, but-" Brandon started talking without turning back to face me.

"Brandon. Stop. Look at me."

He turned around, inch by inch, dragging his eyes across the floor and up the bed before they met mine. His cheeks were beet red and his eyes glistened.

"You don't have to say a single word. Just because she wrote us a note doesn't change anything. While I appreciate her blessing for whatever it's worth, I don't expect anything from you. I will not suddenly start climbing all over you or hitting on you. Promise."

"Here's the thing Jenna. I want to be close to you. I'm lonely; I miss her like crazy. I value the time we spend together more than anything else on Earth right now. I just wouldn't ever want there to be some sort of rebound fling where we come together because we are hurting. Plus, you have Carter and..."

I used a gentle tone for my response. "Brandon, I get it. We really are passengers in the same boat. You've been my lifeline. And if the future finds us in a different place, then we'll see how it goes. But for now, we have each other in the place we need to be and there is no reason to try and turn it into anything else, okay?"

His sigh sounded like it came from the depths of his soul, and his whole body deflated as it released.

"Thank you. Thank you for understanding."

"Good, now that we got that out of the way can we see what they brought us for breakfast? I'm getting hungry."

He laughed, a welcome change from his previous concern. "At least you have your priorities in order. Let's see what she had sent for us."

He began lifting the lids off the dishes and lovely smells wafted out. They were enticing enough to pull me from my place in bed, in spite of being cozy in the covers.

She sent champagne and an assortment of juices, different kinds of pastries and a miniature buffet of warm selections as well. We loaded our plates and spent the next hour talking, drinking mimosas and stuffing ourselves silly.

We opened the box with the bow to find a birthday cake inside. She had even had it inscribed with "Happy Birthday Cassie!"

For some reason that set both of us off and we laughed until we cried. I held my sides as I curled up on the bed, tears rolling down my cheeks.

"I'm gonna wet my pants..."

I staggered from my bed to the bathroom still giggling. I could hear Brandon still chuckling through the closed door. As I washed my hands I took the opportunity to splash some cold water on my face and wash away any trace of the tears that had been falling.

As I returned I flopped backwards onto the bed and let out a deep sigh. "I needed that. I don't laugh nearly enough."

"She was something else, wasn't she? And you know what? I had zero clue that she had any of this up her sleeve. She never even so much as hinted at it.

Sneaky wench." He smiled fondly.

"I didn't know either. Of course, it would have ruined the surprise, but still. Usually, I'm the co-culprit in all her secret stuff. This time I got left out in the cold."

"And she thought of everything. Planned it all down to the last detail."

"Her plans have definitely been thorough."

We spent a moment in silence before he asked what I wanted to do before the show tonight. Today was our last full day, although we didn't take off until the afternoon on Monday.

The day passed quickly and we returned to the room to get ready for dinner and the show. She had booked the late show this time so our plans were to grab dinner, do the trip up the Eiffel Tower and then take a cab to the show.

"Do you just want to eat at the Eiffel Tower restaurant, which will put us halfway up the tower already?"

He nodded. "That works for me."

I chose a pretty jumpsuit that Cassie would have loved, and a pair of the shoes I bought when we got here. My hair got special attention and I bothered with makeup for the first time on this trip. I even added jewelry. All in all, when looking in the mirror at my reflection I felt damn good about myself.

"Woohoo... look at you!" Brandon whistled as I left the bathroom, making me blush.

"She would have been disappointed if I didn't go all out for her."

"And she'd be absolutely ecstatic to see you now."

For a moment I felt self-conscious, wondering if I was doing this for Cassie or for me. Not that it mattered, we both would have wanted the same end result. She had been my biggest cheerleader for our whole lives.

"You look pretty handsome yourself, sir." His perfectly broken-in jeans fit him to a T and the button-down shirt accentuated his muscular physique. "You are indeed worthy of being my date this evening."

"Well thank goodness, I don't know who else you'd go with."

"Are you saying I couldn't find a date?" I teased him.

"Well, you certainly couldn't find one that would live up to my level of perfection," he teased me right back.

"Touche, you are most likely correct."

"Oh, I'm absolutely correct, and you know it." He offered his arm as we headed for the door.

Luckily he had thought to call ahead for reservations and we got one of the remaining few for the evening. We had plenty of time to walk and took a leisurely stroll down the strip, looking at the lights and watching the people as we passed them by.

Everything we ate for dinner tasted amazing. Our server anticipated our every need and suggested the most amazing wine.

The photographer came around to take our photo, as they do everywhere else in Las Vegas. She had us scoot our chairs closer together, and she wanted Brandon to put his arm around me. He settled for draping it across the back of my chair. Both of us balked when she asked if he wanted to kiss my cheek.

"That's plenty, thank you so much." She smiled and headed to the next table over.

He scooted his chair back to his plate. "They sure operate on the assumption that every single pair of people they see is a couple, don't they?"

I grinned. "Well, in their defense, I'd guess that the majority of them are. Or are about to be up close and personal at some point within their trip here."

When the waitress came back to offer dessert both of us declined, citing the cake back in our hotel room. Brandon paid the will while I took care of the photos (because of course I had to buy them all).

On our way to take the elevator up to the top of the tower, we had another pit stop for even more souvenir pictures. Again, we had to explain that we weren't a couple, just friends to get the photographer to ease up on trying to pose us romantically.

The elevator to the top took a few minutes in a fairly crowded little box. When we reached the observation deck and stepped out onto the platform the wind swirled around us. The sun had set and all the lights of the strip shined bright.

Brandon checked the time and announced we only had three or four minutes until the fountains went off again. I couldn't wait. We had a great view from our terrace at the hotel but the tower provided a straight-on view instead of off to the side.

We found a spot at the railing just as the music

came on and the lights began. You could hear the song perfectly from all the way up top and it enhanced a beautiful show.

At the conclusion, we caught the elevator back down.

"Do you want to grab a cab back to the room? Are you cold?" Brandon glanced at my bare arms.

"I don't think I'll be cold but I am getting tired. A cab would be nice." My shoes were new and my feet were beginning to protest.

"You got it, princess." He winked at me and led me towards the lobby where we could grab a ride.

Stopping on the way out we put some money in a slot machine, just for fun. After all, how could you make a trip to Vegas and not gamble even a little tiny bit.

Brandon lost every penny he put in, and I wound up winning a mini jackpot of just over a thousand dollars! I squealed in joy; I never, ever won anything. We made a detour to the ticket machine to get my money and he teased me about wanting to keep gambling since I'd been lucky once already.

"Nope, I'll quit while I'm ahead, thank you very much."

The cab ride back to the hotel took only minutes, in spite of the traffic, and we made it back to our room rather quickly.

"Ready for cake?"

"If you'll give me a minute to get my pajamas on?"

He nodded and set about gathering plates and silverware. I came out to find the table set with the cake and champagne.

We sat together and I looked at him. "We have to sing her happy birthday."

"If you want."

"And I want to make a video of it. For the memory."

I got my phone set up and the two of us sang happy birthday to my very best friend and his late wife, both of us in tears by the end. He cut the cake as I poured the champagne and we had a moment of silence. Lifting my glass, I made a toast to her.

"To Cassie, I miss you more than words will ever have the capability to convey. I know you are watching over me, and I will see you again someday. I love you."

"To my lovely wife. Nothing will ever be the same without you. I'll be waiting until we can meet again as well. I love you."

Our glasses clinked and we took a sip. The cake was amazing and we both ate a large slice. We talked and talked, about anything and everything.

Before I knew it time had passed and I felt my eyes getting drowsy.

"It's bedtime."

"You're right, it sure is. Night Jenna."

We put the rest of the cake in the tiny fridge and left everything where it sat on the table. It would still be there for us to pick up tomorrow.

Chapter Fifteen

We spent our last day in Vegas being lazy. Thanks to Brandon lending me a little of his suitcase space for all my new clothes, I didn't have to go buy one. The zipper bulged and I had to sit on mine to get it closed, but we managed it.

Leaving our luggage in the room we went for one last stroll down the Strip. We grabbed breakfast and Brandon put the kibosh on my doing any more shopping, citing the lack of real estate left in either suitcase. We took a stroll through Siegfried and Roy's

Secret Garden. Dolphins had always been some of my favorite animals to watch.

We enjoyed them so much that after touring the rest of the exhibits we returned and ate lunch at the snack shack, sitting at the poolside table watching them play until we needed to head back to catch our limo to the airport.

We sat quietly on the short ride to the airport, both of us lost in our own thoughts. The weekend away had recharged my batteries and made me feel more like my old self. I didn't relish the idea of going home and having a tough conversation with Carter, but it needed to be done. Brandon wasn't going anywhere, and if he couldn't get past his jealousy and see that then we probably weren't going anywhere together either.

The airport bustled with travelers coming and going, but the line through security didn't take too long. Once we got close to our gate both of us sat down and put some money into a lost machine to pass the time.

Neither of us won anything, go figure, and I printed my leftover ticket out to take home as a souvenir. It had a whopping $.79 on it.

On the plane, I settled in with a glance of wine and

looked at Brandon. "I can't fly first class any more. I'm going to get too used to this and we all know I won't be flying first class for the rest of my life!"

He chuckled. "Why not? It's the best way to fly."

"Because I'm cheap and I'd rather save all that extra money for doing fun things, or the next trip."

He shrugged. "Wherever your priorities lie, that's all that matters. You do you. Let me tell you, though, when it's a long international flight, first class is still the way to go. Nine hours or more in one of those cramped seats back there is no picnic."

"Well, if I ever get the opportunity to take one of those flights I will keep your advice in mind."

The flight passed uneventfully and before I knew it we were grabbing our luggage from the carousel and heading out to the parking garage.

The weather didn't look anything like the Las Vegas we had just left and made me glad I had worn a sweater. The wind blew through the concrete levels and you could feel the dampness from the rain outside. Leaving the garage led us straight into a winter deluge of water from the angry looking clouds above.

Heat blaring and windshield wipers thwacking we

navigated our way across town and back to my place.

As he pulled into the drive I looked over at him. "Don't get out, I'll just grab my suitcase and run."

"What about all the stuff you have in mine?"

"I'll catch you sometime this week and come get it if that's okay? I know Toby will be excited to see you and I don't want to take too much of your time."

"Okay." He paused. "I had such a good time this weekend, Jenna. You have no idea how healing it's been for me."

Our eyes met.

"Oh, but I do. I feel more like my old self than I have all year. I don't know how she knew how much we would need this, but she did, and I am ever so grateful. Thank you for an amazing weekend."

He reached across and pulled me into a one-armed hug. "Thank you."

As he released me I gathered my purse, digging out my keys in preparation. I only had a short run to my tiny covered porch but it was really coming down.

"Here I go, wish me luck!"

I jumped out and rushed to get my suitcase from the back seat, laughing as the rain soaked my hair and ran down my face. I made a mad dash across the cobblestone walkway, turning to wave once I reached cover.

Brandon waved back and sat in the drive until I had the door open, ensuring I got inside safely before he put it in reverse and drove away. Using the suitcase to block an escape attempt I scooted inside, immediately leaving a wet spot on the entryway rug.

Kate jumped into my arms, only to turn around and jump right back out when she discovered the water soaking every inch of me. She sat at a safe distance and meowed her displeasure, licking herself to remove the offending liquid.

I shook my head at her. "Sorry kitty, it's pouring out there."

After a trip to the bathroom to grab a towel and slip into my robe, I headed for the kitchen. Neither of us had been very hungry on the flight, but now that I was home my stomach growled. A note from my sister lay on the counter next to a bouquet of flowers in a vase.

Her note assured me that Kate had been fine the whole weekend and everything had gone as planned. At the bottom of the note, she had scribbled another short message, explaining that Carter had come by and delivered the flowers.

That caught me by surprise. I had assumed they were another piece of Cassie's prearranged birthday plans. I plucked the little white envelope from its plastic trident and opened it. The little card held only three words.

I'm sorry. ~Carter

Well, well, well. Maybe things would work out between us after all. I decided to eat and shower before calling him.

By the time I had finished showering, I just wanted to go to bed. I carried my phone with me as I walked through the house locking up and double-checking the doors and windows, debating whether or not I should text him.

Deciding I at least owed him a thank you for the flowers, I sent a short text letting him know that I was going to bed and turning off my phone so I would text him in the morning.

I climbed into bed and Kate curled up next to me, purring loudly. Apparently she had forgiven me both for being gone and for getting her wet when I returned. The weekend replayed in my mind as I lay there, cementing how thankful I was for Cassie, even though she was no longer with us.

My thoughts turned to her birthday note. I had been shocked that she insinuated Brandon and I should begin dating. Not as shocked as he had been, judging by his reaction, but still quite caught off guard. I didn't think I could ever date my dead best friend's husband. That would just be too weird. Wouldn't it?

I drifted off to sleep thinking about how much fun I had had with him over the weekend, how comfortable and safe I felt with him, then sternly reminding myself that I had a man. Carter and I may have only been dating for a couple of months, but I shouldn't be entertaining even the thought of anyone else. Brandon may have been a hard act to live up to, even as a friend, but he still loved Cassie.

The storms from the day before gave way to a quiet morning. The air smelled clean and fresh, the temperature not so chilly that I couldn't open my windows a crack while I picked up the house a bit before settling down to work a few hours.

It might have been petty, but I decided to put off

calling Carter until I finished my hours for the day. Flowers made for a nice apology, but I didn't want him getting the idea that they would automatically fix something whenever he decided to be an ass.

Turns out, I didn't have to call him. He sent me a text just as I finished up my last bit of data entry for the day, asking if he had permission to call or stop by. He offered to bring dinner by so we could talk. I accepted.

He knocked on the door about an hour later, carryout bags and a bottle of wine in his hands. I let him in, standing quietly to the side with a wriggling Kate in my arms. He gave me a sideways glance and headed for the dining room as I followed behind.

He held out the bottle of wine. "I really am sorry, Jenna."

"Here's the thing, Carter. I thought about this for a long time last night while I should have been sleeping. Brandon isn't going anywhere. Ever. He and I were good friends before Cassie died, and we are even closer now. He will always be a part of my life. And if you can't bring yourself to accept that, and not be childish about it, then the two of us have nothing to look forward to. I don't want to date someone who acts like you did over this weekend. Period."

At least he had the good grace to look embarrassed, casting his eyes to the floor before looking back up to meet mine. He exhaled loudly.

"I understand." He pointed to his forehead. "Here, I understand." He tapped on his chest, right over his heart. "Here, though, it's hard. To know the girl I am dating went off to spend a romantic weekend with someone that wasn't me."

"It wasn't-" I started.

"Wait please." He held up a hand. "No matter what the intentions were, flying away with each other and staying in a hotel suite, separate beds or not is romantic because it wasn't a business trip. You saw shows together, went out to dinner together and did countless things together while you were there, just the two of you. Things *I* would have liked to do with you."

He paused and I stayed silent, waiting to see if he had anything more to say. After another deep breath, he continued.

"The two of you already have a special bond. I get it. But sometimes those are the foundations that lead to more. It happens all the time. I just don't want to get deeper into this with you to have you fall for him down the road."

"Carter. I get it. I do. And this kind of adult conversation is constructive, we will need to have quite a few more of them, I'm sure. But I will not put up with the childish behavior from this weekend no matter what the reason. Brandon was married to my best friend. His *wife* just died a few short months ago. Who happened to be my best friend. We are still grieving. It hurts. On a visceral level."

I took a deep breath. I didn't want to cry during this conversation because it would affect the tone of our discussion. I wasn't crying over us, and that's what we needed to be focused on.

"His presence soothes that. For me, spending time with those who were closest to her helps the pain. I won't apologize for that, and I won't give it up. For anyone. And if you think you are going to ask me to, then we might want to take a break for a little bit. Maybe I'm not ready to be dipping my toes into the dating pool yet. With anybody."

"Jenna, don't say that. Give us another chance. I already said I'm sorry."

"Yes, you did. But you haven't addressed the behavior itself, and whether that will change. When I tell you that I will be going to Brandon's next weekend, to have brunch, and see Toby, and get some stuff from him that I packed into his suitcase due to lack of space in mine, am I going to get an attitude? Will you be upset over that too? Because I simply cannot deal with that."

"I am going to try. I will give it one hundred percent of my best effort. I promise you that."

I sighed. Knowing in my head that it might not be good enough, I decided to let the matter drop. One day at a time. I did want to have a nice evening with him. Id' missed him while away and had looked forward to spending time with him again.

"Okay. That's a good start, and the best one can truly promise to another. Should we eat?"

His shoulders relaxed and some of the tension eased from his face. Pulling containers from the bag he began opening them one by one. Indian food from Cassie and my favorite restaurant.

We sat on the couch and talked as we ate, leaving the television off and focusing on each other. Kate kept trying to steal my chicken.

"Shoo, naughty kitty." I waved my chopsticks at her.

"You know, you still owe me dinner, seeing as how it's been how many weeks, and she's obviously still here." He winked at me.

"I suppose I do. When would you like to collect?"

"Let's go out Friday night? If you aren't busy of course."

"I'm not, so that works. Think about where you want to go."

The rest of the evening passed rather pleasantly. We snuggled up close and watched a movie and talked about the upcoming Christmas holiday. He explained that he always flew out to be with his parents for the week of Christmas and New Year's, apologizing because this year's ticket had already been purchased.

"Don't worry about it. You don't have to apologize for spending time with your family. We can work something out."

"We won't get to spend New Year's Eve together though." He almost looked pouty at the thought.

"There's always next year."

He agreed, and we made plans to get together the

Saturday night before he flew out. The rest of the evening passed pleasantly, and he left about ten.

I walked him to the door to say goodnight and he kissed me deeply. "I could stay a little longer," he hinted.

I laughed it off, not sure why I didn't want him to stay. "Another time. I'm exhausted."

A smile was his only response as he walked out the door, waving as he got into the car. The air outside gave me the chills and I closed the door before Kate got out, realizing I wouldn't be able to go to sleep yet.

I took the last glass of wine and had a soak in the tub, hoping to both relax my body and clear my head. I sure needed it.

Chapter Sixteen

The work-week passed quickly as I attempted to make my list for Christmas shopping so I could get it finished. While I usually loved the act of gathering gifts for everyone, Cassie and I had been making a weekend of it ever since we were old enough to drive, and the memories were swamping me.

It always involved lots of food and fun, and a sleepover no matter what age we were, in addition to the shopping. We took everything back to a central location and then spent the next day wrapping everything, listening to Christmas carols and drinking hot chocolate. This year I planned to go alone, and I wanted to do it all in one trip.

This coming weekend I also needed to get my tree up. Even though we never had Christmas morning at my place I loved to see it through my front window as I drove up to the house. Twinkling lights and shiny decorations always made me smile.

Kate came sliding sideways across my desk, knocking my pen to the floor and I worried about how she would take to the tree. I might have to leave any fragile and important ornaments in the box this year to prevent a tragedy.

I'd worked enough during the week to take Friday off for shopping, hoping that even though I had gotten perilously close to the holiday enough people would still be at work and the crowds would be manageable.

I bundled up, took my list, and headed out to the mall. There were a few things I had been able to order online, but for Christmas I liked the search. Touching the items and holding them in my hand gave me a better idea if they suited the person I wanted to purchase them for.

I had lunch in the food court, staring off into space at the bustling crowds and festive decorations. A hand on my shoulder startled me out of my reverie.

"Earth to Jenna?"

"Aye! Hi, Dana. How have you been? Sit down for a bit." I hadn't seen her since her birthday party a couple months before, the one where I had met Carter at the bar. We'd texted a couple times but never managed to sync our schedules.

"Fine, and thanks. What about you? Doing your shopping?"

"Trying to." I indicated the small pile at my feet. "I've been at it all day already and this is all I have to show for my efforts. Nothing seems to meet the picture in my head." I realized how much Cassie had driven my choices in the past. She always had an opinion or a suggestion.

"Don't stress about it too much. Christmas is supposed to be a happy time. I've got my last few right here." She held up the few bags hanging from her arm.

"That's definitely a reason to be happy. I'm not leaving here until I have all my presents. Or the mall closes and security kicks me out."

"So how's everything else? Things with Carter? And how's Brandon?"

"Fine, okay, and he's doing good."

She laughed. "Well, don't overwhelm me with the details or anything. I mean, I would have *asked* if I had any interest, ya know?"

My turn to giggle. "Sorry. Most things are fine. Stuff with Carter is complicated. He is insanely jealous of Brandon. Which causes trouble for us, because I told him that Brandon isn't going anywhere."

Dana raised her brows. "What's up between you and Brandon?"

"Nothing. That's the thing." I sighed. "He is just jealous over the place he has in my life. I don't know. I tried explaining it to him, but I don't think he really understood."

"Maybe he'll get over it?" Dana looked about as convinced as I felt.

"I think it may just be a personality trait of his. We'll see though. He promised to work on it."

We chatted for a few more minutes before I looked at my phone and realized I needed to get moving if I had any hope of finishing my shopping today.

"Are you done, or do you want to hit some stores with me?"

"I'm done, but I'm parked on the far side of the mall, so if you are headed that way I will wander a few stores with you on my way out."

By the time we hit the far exit I had managed to get everything on my list except for a gift for Brandon.

"Not bad. Thanks for all your help, and your company, Dana."

"Any time. It was so great to see you." We stopped

next to her car, which happened to be just a few down from my own. "And think about coming to the Christmas party, okay? I'm going to ask Brandon too."

"I'll think about it. I promise."

We hugged awkwardly, working around my arms full of bags as best we could. She drove past as I tucked my bags in the trunk, waiting to be sure I got into my car before waving and driving off.

I headed towards home, thankful to be almost done and actually looking forward to the wrapping. Just as I got off my exit I heard a loud pop and my car jerked forcefully to the right. Luckily nothing was over there but the shoulder, but it was fairly dark on this stretch of the off-ramp.

Exiting the car to inspect the damage, I cussed out loud. Sure enough, I had a flat tire. I called Triple A just to be told the had about a two hour wait time for assistance. Leaning my head against the steering wheel I grumbled, then dug out my phone.

"Hey you," Brandon answered on the first ring.

"I'm so glad you answered."

"Of course I did. What's wrong?"

"I've got a flat. I'm just on the shoulder at the exit, but it's so dark I don't feel safe getting out and trying to change it and Triple A has at least a two-hour wait."

"Sit in the car with your flashers on, I'm on my way."

After verifying the exit, he hung up and I waited for him to arrive. He must not have wasted any time because it seemed like he made it in no time flat. I got out as he walked up to the trunk.

I hugged him. "Thank you for coming."

"No thanks needed. Let's get you fixed up."

I moved my purchases to the back seat so he could get at the spare tire, while he went to get the "real" jack from the back of his truck. Less than ten minutes later he had the spare on and the jack and my busted tire in the back of his truck.

"You'll definitely need a new one, maybe a pair if

the other one is too old. Do you need me to come with you?"

"Nah, I don't think so, thanks. But I will call you if I change my mind. Thanks again. I can't tell you how much I appreciate this."

He just shook his head. "I told you, you don't have to thank me. Now get in so we can get off this dark exit. I'll follow you home."

"You don't have to-"

"Ah. Shh. Get in the car. Let's go." He gently steered me to the door and opened it for me.

Thanks to the minimal traffic on the road we made it to my place fairly quickly and he pulled into the drive behind me.

"Want to come in for coffee or wine? We could order take out or something?"

"Sure, I can stay for a few minutes."

After helping me carry all my bags in, which made me grateful I hadn't found something for him this trip, we made a pot of coffee and settled on the couch.

"How are you doing?"

His fingers drummed quietly as he held his coffee cup. "Not bad. The rapid succession of important dates kind of messes with my head, but I think I'm managing. And you?"

"About the same. I did my Christmas shopping without her for the first time in years today. It hurt, but I made it through. I ran into Dana, who invited me to her holiday party. She said she wants you to come too."

"Yeah, she called and left a voicemail. Are you going?"

"I'm thinking about it. Told her I would consider it but didn't commit."

We sat in silence for a minute.

"Are you putting up a tree?"

He shook his head. "I don't think so. Not this year."

"Want to come over and help me do mine? You can bring whatever I left in your suitcase and I can be in charge of brunch this week?"

"Why not? It will be fun, right?"

"Of course, aren't I always fun?" I scrunched up my facc as if daring him to contradict me.

"Yes, yes you are. But I better go before Toby starts to think I got lost. He'll be happy to get over here and acquaint himself with Kate again."

We both laughed. "Much happier than she will probably be."

Out hug lasted a long time, both of us drawing on the other for strength. These first holidays were always the worst, but we'd make it through.

"Thanks again. Have a good night, drive safe, and I'll see you Sunday!"

Once Brandon was out of the driveway I closed the door and sat Kate down. In spite of my debacle with the tire, the shopping trip really hadn't gone all that badly. I had most of the gifts I needed and I had picked up wrapping paper, bows, and gift bags so I would be prepared to get them all ready for giving when the time came.

Deciding that I was too tired to wrap them tonight I stuck them all in my closet and left them for another day. Not ready to go to bed quite yet, I headed out to the garage to take out all of the Christmas decorations down from their storage space, where they spent the majority of the year. I had an artificial tree but decided next year I wanted to go get a fresh one. After about an hour, I had managed to drag all of the bins that held the decorations into the house..

The outside lights would have to wait, perhaps Brandon would be willing to help me put them up on Sunday. In the meantime, I started pulling things out of the bins and spreading them out across the couch so that I could see what I had and what I wanted to put out. I decided to leave my Christmas houses in their boxes this year, just in case Kate took a particular interest in them. I would be sad if they got broken. Many of them were collectibles that would be hard to replace after this many years.

Kate was happy playing with all the bubble wrap, wrapping paper and other odds and ends that I left on the floor for her. That entertained her enough that I was able to go through the important things without being bothered too much. Of course, like all cats, she was most interested in the empty boxes and wound up curling up in one to take a nap.

I began setting out the festive decorations, losing track of time. Before I knew it the clock struck midnight and I still hadn't gone to bed. I needed to get some sleep! Leaving Kate in her box since she was still sound asleep, I headed back to my bedroom, hoping for a good night's rest.

I'd managed to work myself to exhaustion, and slept straight through the night with no disruptions. I was quite surprised to sit up the next morning and see that the clock read nine. I almost never slept that late.

At some point, Kate must have come in to join me on the bed, and I left her sleeping there on the pillow as I went to find breakfast. I debated whether to call or text Carter and see if he wanted to come by at some point today. Part of me felt like I wanted to spend the day alone wrapping my gifts. The other part of me knew that I would do well with some distraction from being sad about not having Cassie next to me while I did it.

In the end, I decided to send him a text while I had my coffee. He sent a response letting me know that he'd be busy for most of the day that he'd come by this afternoon. That gave me a few hours to get my wrapping done, do a little more decorating, and have some time to myself.

In spite of my desire to have time for myself, I

started feeling lonely before breakfast was even finished. Kate came out to join me, but she didn't have the same conversational skills as another human being. I needed someone to sit and talk with me so I could work through my feelings of not having Cassie. Her birthday had been bad but I had a feeling that Christmas was going to be even worse.

I managed to keep myself from texting Brandon and instead gave my mom a call. she was glad to hear from me and it made me feel better that I had taken the time to reach out to her. I knew that I had been neglecting my parents since losing Cassie and it wasn't fair to them. I just didn't have a whole lot of extra energy for socialization, even for my own parents. I knew they missed me, though, and we set up plans to get together during the next week.

After hanging up from my mom, I did feel better. The rest of the day went by fairly quickly as I got my house ready for Christmas. I changed the linens on the dining table, adding a table runner and a cute Christmas centerpiece. I hung holiday decor on the walls and changed out the rugs for Christmassy ones. If it hadn't been for the pouring rain outside, I would have gone out and done the yard stakes and some of the other outdoor decorations.

By the time Carter texted that he was ready to head

over, I had done most of the things that I had set out to do that day except the wrapping. I had gotten so caught up in decorating that I ran out of time. Tomorrow was another day. Maybe I'd text Brandon and tell him to bring whatever gifts he needed to wrap and we could do it together.

Leaving Kate to play with the packing paper and empty boxes, I headed back to take a shower and at least make an attempt to look pretty for Carter. I left the Christmas music playing and made sure the bathroom door stayed open so I could hear it while I was showering.

I dressed in jeans and a red sweater, even putting on my Christmas. We might be a couple of weeks out from Christmas but I felt like getting in the holiday mood.

Chapter Seventeen

Carter showed up at the door holding a box from Francesca's Bakery in his hands. "I'd seen enough of her boxes sitting on the kitchen counter that I knew you enjoyed her cooking. I didn't know what your favorite treats are, though, so I just got a selection of everything."

"Carter, that is so sweet of you. I like just about everything she makes, so I'm sure I will enjoy whatever is in the box. Come on in."

"Wow, Jenna. I see you've been doing some

decorating."

"I have! It's one of my favorite times of the year, even though this year has been harder without Cassie. I did my best to spend my time doing something I enjoyed and to use it to get me in the holiday spirit."

"Well, it looks great. Do you need any help putting up the outside decorations?"

"Right now I'm just going to leave them in the bins, thanks to the weather. They're not worth going outside and getting soaked."

"Well, if the weather lightens up and you'd like my help let me know. Are you hungry? Do we want to order something for dinner?"

"I put lasagna in the oven earlier, and I've got some garlic bread here. Does that sound okay to you?"

"Sure. I like lasagna."

We had about fifteen minutes until dinner came out of the oven and I decided to use it to get the wine ready. I put the bakery box on the counter so we could have whatever was inside for dessert.

"What are you doing tomorrow Jenna? Do you have any plans?"

"Yes, Carter." I sighed, unsure of whether or not I

should share my plans or let it go. "You know on Sundays Brandon and I have brunch. He's bringing Toby and coming over here. We're going to wrap our Christmas gifts together. "

I caught the quick shift of Carter's expression before he was able to hide it. I knew he was frustrated to hear me say that I'd be doing holiday things with Brandon, instead of him. At first, he didn't voice anything out loud which I took to be a good sign. However, until dinner was ready he didn't speak another word.

"Carter, is there a problem?" I asked.

"You know how I feel about you being so close to him, and yet you make it a point to let me know that you will be spending time with Brandon and doing holiday things with him, instead of with me. I don't know what you want me to say to you or how you want me to behave."

I sighed, inhaling deeply through my nose and exhaling through my mouth, trying to keep my patience.

"Listen, Carter. You asked if I had plans tomorrow. I do. I didn't want you to think I was hiding anything from you, because there is nothing to hide. So I told you what my plans were. Please don't ask me if you were going to get upset when I am honest with you. "

It was his turn to sigh. He couldn't look me in the eyes, pretending to be focused on opening a bottle of wine and pouring us each glass. I could see that he was struggling in spite of his promise to not make such a big deal out of things.

"Carter. Look at me please."

He brought his eyes from the glass of wine he was holding and met mine. I could see he was doing his best to school the look on his face into something more appropriate, but he was failing. He looked angry, and I, in turn, got angry that he dared to be angry with me.

"I am beginning to fear that you really are not going to be able to adjust to this and let it go."

His jaw clenched, and I could see him swallow. "I don't know either, but I am trying."

"If this is going to bother you so much, maybe we are just wasting our time. I don't want this relationship to become more stress than it is joy."

He shook his head before I had even finished my sentence. "That's not fair. You haven't even really given me a chance. I am *trying* to learn to accept it. But it's not going to happen overnight. I've never had this problem in a relationship before."

I felt bad because he had a point. "Okay, can we let it go for tonight then, and just enjoy our evening? You leave next weekend for Christmas at your parents, and I don't want to go in the holiday made at each other. Deal?"

He finished filling the glass he had been holding and handed it to me. "Deal."

The rest of the evening passed without any bickering, but I could feel the underlying tension that made it uncomfortable. He got up to leave about eight, long before he usually headed home, and didn't even hint at being invited to stay the night – thank goodness.

He left with a quick peck on my cheek and a promise to text me the following evening some time.

"Drive safe, it's getting icy out there."

He raised his hand in acknowledgment but didn't respond. Shaking my head I closed the door behind him and went to clean up the kitchen, talking to Kate as I did.

"Can you believe the nerve of that man? Or boy, rather. He's acting like a spoiled little boy who's not getting his way."

I fumed as I wiped the counters and put the leftovers away.

"Who does he think he is anyways? I have every right to bc fricnds with whomever I choose, And I will spend time with whomever I please."

Kate sat on the kitchen floor, watching me curiously but not interrupting my monologue.

"And another thing! It's not like I give him a hard time about anyone he wants to spend time with. Most of the time I don't even ask. It's about trust. He doesn't trust me and that makes me so angry!"

I threw the sponge in the sink and slammed the dishwasher door closed with more force than was necessary.

"You can bet that if Brandon helps me put the lights up tomorrow he is going to get all butt-hurt over that the next time he comes over too. I don't need this hassle. It's almost Christmas damn it."

Kate finally meowed, drawing my attention to the fact that her bowl sat empty.

"Ugh. Sorry girl. Let me fill it for you. Thanks for listening to me rant and rave a like a crazy woman."

Hearing the words come out of my mouth gave me pause. Should I really be trying to cultivate a relationship with someone who made me rant and rave at all? Is this what I wanted for my love life? I thought about what would Cassie have said if she had been the one listening to my woes, instead of a kitten.

Deciding to let it go for the evening to give myself time to cool off, I promised myself I would revisit the issue with a much cooler temper the next evening. Early to bed seemed like the best plan for now. As I lay there I let random thoughts run through my head. Dating sucked. Maybe I just wouldn't do it at all.

My early bedtime led me to be wide awake just before five the next morning. After fifteen unsuccessful minutes of pleading with myself to go back to sleep I gave up, grumbling as I climbed out of bed. Why oh why did I have to be up before the sun on a Sunday?

After a shower, I decided to put my hours before brunch to work. I made biscuit dough from scratch, ready to pop into the oven just before we wanted to eat. I prepped potatoes for homemade roasted red potato hash browns and set all the ingredients for hollendaise sauce out to come to room temperature.

Then I gathered all the gift wrapping supplies I could find. Tape, ribbon, bows, tags, scissors, you name it. I put some hot cocoa in the crock pot to go with our coffee and orange juice.

Every gift I had purchased on my shopping spree made it to the dining room and I set about removing price tags, humming along to the Christmas station I had turned on as I went.

I had just enough time to snatch Kate up when I heard the door to Brandon's truck thump shut from the driveway. Opening the door allowed Toby to come bounding through before Brandon had even made it up the walk. Kate hissed, jumped from my arms and took off down the hall. I had to laugh.

Brandon squeezed past me with his bags full of gifts.

"I set everything out in the dining room for wrapping, so you can take them in there," I informed him as I latched the door shut. "It means we'll have to have breakfast amongst the mess, but I find the table the most comfortable place to wrap."

"Works for me," he agreed with a wink.

"I prepped everything, so I'll just get started if you

want to start wrapping."

"You don't have your outside lights up? Why not?" He seemed surprised.

"Because it has been so wet, I didn't feel like going out to put them up."

"Where's the ladder? I'll throw them up while you make breakfast. Seems like fair trade to me."

"You don't have to do that!" I tried to tell him he didn't need to go outside and put the lights up, but he wasn't hearing it.

"Jenna, come on. It'll only take me about fifteen minutes. It's not like your house is that big. By the time I get back in, breakfast should be ready and we can eat."

I smiled to myself waving towards the garage door. "Okay. And yes, the ladder is in the garage on the far wall. Thank you."

He made his way through the door to the garage telling Toby to stay as he did. I busied myself frying the potatoes and poaching the eggs. The sauce would go on at the very last minute. The hot chocolate smelled heavenly, and I almost decided to have it instead of coffee. Almost.

Brandon had been correct. He was done stringing

the lights on the roof before I even had breakfast finished. I was still poaching the eggs and stirring the sauce when he came back in.

We sat down to eat, talking about whatever we had missed since the last time we saw each other. I made Toby a couple of poached eggs and he said happily eating them in his bowl beside the table.

We spent our time chit-chatting and having brunch, not at all in a rush. It was the best way to start a Sunday, in spite of the fact that I had been up since before dawn. There was nothing better than eating good food, relaxing with good company, and enjoying the moment.

Once we finished eating I threw the dishes in the sink, telling Brandon not to worry about them. I wanted to get to the gift wrapping. He pulled the things he had purchased out and made his own pile, as I started on mine.

Watching him wrap his first gift, I had to laugh. He was the quintessential male, unable to make a nice corner or an unwrinkled package. And the look on his face when I asked him if he was going to tie it with a ribbon? Hilarious.

Finally, I took pity on him. "Brandon! Leave it be.

How about you sit here and keep me company, while I wrap the gifts? I'll do both yours and mine, and you can make it up to me later."

Brandon threw up his hands. "Are you insulting my gift wrapping technique?"

I threw a bow at him, laughing. "You can't expect me to believe that you are going to wrap that whole pile of gifts with that type of presentation, and then give them to your family and friends for Christmas."

"What? Why not?"

"Hands off the scissors and the tape, Brandon. From here on out it looks like I'll be the only one doing the wrapping. It will be your job to keep my coffee cup full with coffee or cocoa, and you can hand me them and tell me whose name goes on the tag."

"You do realize we could be here all day, right?"

"Do you have anywhere else to be today?"

"Actually, I don't. I was just thinking of you. Do you really want to spend an entire day wrapping gifts, half of which aren't even yours?"

"I actually love wrapping gifts. It is one of the highlights of the holiday season for me. That's why I save them all up and do them at one time. I turn on the

Christmas music, have some hot cocoa and enjoy myself."

"Well, if you enjoy it so much who am I to deny you the pleasure of wrapping all these gifts?"

Our estimation of it taking an entire day turned out to be slightly exaggerated. It only took me a couple of hours to get all of the gifts beautifully wrapped. I collected wrapping paper, usually spending the day after Christmas going in and buying up the ones that went on clearance to add to my stash for the next year. I had ribbons and bows galore. Even my gift tags matched the wrapping paper. Everything coordinated perfectly.

When Brandon's gifts were ready for giving, I made sure they all got bagged up and sat by the front door so he wouldn't forget them.

"Is there anything else we need to get done today?"

Brandon shook his head. "I don't think so. Is there anywhere you would like to go? Anything you would like to do? The rest of my day is yours, I owe you for wrapping all of my gifts."

"I'm going to consider us even since you hung on my outside lights."

"So, what are your plans for Christmas Eve and

Christmas Day?" Brandon asked.

"Well, I think I'm going to go to my parents on Christmas morning. I don't want to spend the night over there Christmas Eve like I usually do, so I will probably just be here at home."

"Do you want to come with me on Christmas Eve? We are all going to Liam and Amanda's. We will have a great big dinner, exchange gifts, and enjoy the evening. We decided to go to their house this year so they didn't have to drag the twins out. It's awfully late for them to be out and about, and of course, the weather is crap in December."

"I'd love to! Are you sure they won't mind me intruding?"

The thought of staying home alone on Christmas Eve had had me down. But I knew, as I'd said to Brandon, that I didn't want to spend the night at my parents' house. I had planned for Kate and I to just sit and have takeout for dinner and enjoy an evening in front of the Christmas tree. Maybe we would watch a couple Christmas movies.

"Amanda absolutely demanded that I invite you, so I'm pretty sure she'd be more upset if you didn't show, then if you did."

"How sweet of her. Thank you so much for asking. As long as you're sure, I would love to join you guys. You'll have to give me some gift ideas for Amanda and Liam, and your parents. I think I can figure the twins out."

"Well, we only have a couple of days left. Do you want to head to the mall and do some Christmas shopping now? Since I'll be tagging along I can give you ideas for everyone."

"That would work out. After that the only person I have left to finish is you!"

"You know you don't have to get me a gift."

"Brandon, shut up. You already know I'm getting you something for Christmas. I can't imagine not getting you anything."

"Will Toby be okay here with Kate, or should we take him home and drop him off?"

I hesitated. I knew Toby would be okay with it, but I'm not sure how Kate would take it. It might be one of those situations where we came back to a trashed house because Toby had decided to chase her all over, just wanting to have fun of course, but she might not take too kindly to it.

"Let me just throw these dishes in the dishwasher, and we can drop him off at your place on our way out. Does that work? I know Toby would be fine here, but I'm not sure about Kate. She might just lose her mind if I left the dog here with her all day with no supervision." I had to laugh at the thought.

Brandon nodded his head. "We will have to set up a time for Toby to come over and spend the night soon, so they can get to know each other a little bit better. She's going to have to learn that Toby will be around for quite a while. "

"Yes, she will. And I think if she gets a little bit older and grows up around him, she's going to be just fine."

For some reason, it warmed my heart that he was willing to say out loud that Toby would be around for a long, long time. I think somewhere in the back of my mind I always had this fear that eventually he would get tired of bringing Toby to me and I would end up losing him.

Chapter Eighteen

The drive to the mall was choked with traffic, and the parking lot wasn't much better. Everybody and their mother seem to be out doing last-minute Christmas shopping. I had been so proud of myself for getting mine done ahead of time, and here I was, shopping some more.

Brandon managed to finagle the truck into a small parking spot on the backside of the mall. Luckily they had an entrance over there. We walked in and I looked at him

"Which store should we hit first? I need to get your mom, your dad, Liam and Amanda, and the twins."

Brandon looked around. "Do you want to hit the baby store first? The twins will be the easiest, and we can just get them out of the way."

I nodded. "Seems as good a place to start as any. Let's go."

We wandered the aisles, picking out gifts for each of the twins. I may have gone a little overboard, and gotten each of them three or four. What could I say? Who doesn't love shopping for babies?

We ran into Cassie's brother and his wife in one of the stores, both of them looking surprised to see Brandon and I together.

"Hey Evan, how've you been? And how is Alicia?"

He looked at me strangely before answering. "Fine, she's fine thanks. I hear you two have been spending a lot of time together lately?"

His tone shocked me, and I couldn't find the words to answer him. Luckily Brandon stepped in.

"Yes, we have. Why?"

Evan gave Brandon a dirty look. "My sister was barely cold in her grave before you started moving on, huh? And you," he glared at me, "some best friend moving in on her husband."

"Evan! It's not like that at all!"

He just shook his head as he started to turn away. "You two make me sick."

I started to follow him, but Brandon grabbed my arm, holding me back. "Leave him be. He's still grieving."

"But... I don't want him to think-" I stopped short. Brandon was right. Hopefully, Evan would come to his senses soon.

In spite of the run-in with Evan, I wanted to enjoy the rest of my shopping trip, and I did my best to put him out of my mind. I made a mental note to talk to her parents the next time I saw them, hoping they weren't getting the same impression as their son.

We continued wandering the stores, buying things for his family. I picked out something and he'd either give it a yay or a nay, meaning I either purchased it or put it back, then moved on to the next thing. In a little under two hours, I had gifts for everybody who needed them, except him of course, and we headed back to my house to do a little more wrapping.

By late afternoon the two of us were getting hungry. I looked at him, "Do you want to order some takeout for dinner, or do you need to get back?"

As we were discussing dinner, my phone dinged. I knew right then that it was a text from Carter. I also knew that at that moment I was just going to ignore it. I didn't want to lie to him, but I also didn't want to start a fight. Brandon and I were enjoying our day and I wasn't going to let him ruin it.

Brandon very politely didn't ask about the text message, and I didn't offer. I knew that he knew exactly what was going on.

We ordered takeout and finished wrapping while we waited for the food to arrive. Kate enjoyed more time with their ribbons and bows and followed us when we moved to the couch to watch some TV.

The rest of the evening was spent very pleasantly cuddled on the couch and eating good food. Brandon stayed until about ten, which was plenty late enough for me, seeing as how I had been up since the butt crack of dawn.

I walked into the door to ensure that he got his bags of gifts and gave him a big hug. "Thank you so much for everything. I love having you here."

"Thanks for having me, you know I love being here. If I don't see you this week, I will call you as soon as I find out what time we need to be at Amanda's on Sunday for Christmas Eve."

"Perfect. Have a good week!"

I could barely believe that we were only a week away from Christmas Eve and that I would get to spend it with his family. Reminding myself that I needed to make it over to see Cassie's parents later in the week as well, I attempted to figure out what I wanted to get Brandon for Christmas. Unfortunately, I drifted off to sleep before settling on anything.

The last week before the holiday was filled with the usual hustle and bustle that came with the time of year. I finally settled on what I considered to be the perfect gift for Brandon, pleased with myself for coming up with it. My gift for Carter, in comparison, seemed lackluster.

We made it all the way to Thursday before I heard from him, and I'd begun to wonder whether we were still on for our Friday night date. His text chimed in at eight, as I contemplated the weather from my patio chair.

The night was cold, and it smelled like snow. I'd

stepped outside just to get a little fresh air after burning the crap out of a batch of scones.

Kate had once again gotten into the Christmas tree, this time managing to get herself stuck in a strand of lights on top of sending the ornaments flying. As I extricated her wriggling body from the cord, I lost track of my timer. Suddenly the smoke alarm blared. Luckily she had been freed, because I jumped to my feet, the ornament mess all but forgotten.

The offending pan of scones had been ripped from the oven with hot pads and tossed onto the back patio. My neighbor, a smoker whose wife didn't allow the habit in the house, could smell the char and laughed at me from his patio.

"I don't need any, Jenna, whatever they are, but thanks for offering!" He teased me.

I laughed out loud. "But, Kevin, I made them specially for you!" I teased right back.

"Probably better than Maggie could do, at any rate."

"Ooh, Kevin, I am telling your wife on you."

"The window's open, she can hear me, and she ain't said nothing because she knows it's true."

I heard Maggie's merry laughter float out from inside. "I won't argue with him on this one, Jenna!"

"I have some that aren't burnt, and I'll send a few over."

Ducking back inside I grabbed a half dozen of the perfectly baked ones and put them on a paper plate, slipping it into a gallon-sized Ziploc bag. Taking it back outside I handed it over to Kevin.

"Here you guys go! Enjoy. I need to take this pan out to the waste bin now that they've quit smoking. Something you should do too, Kevin, it's bad for your health."

I gave him a hard time about it every chance I got, taking over for Cassie now that she couldn't do it. It had been her mission in life to "get him on a healthier path" since the day they met.

I heard him chuckle as I closed the kitchen door. "Okay, Cassie."

The insinuation made me smile, instead of making me sad. She'd be tickled pink to know I had taken up her pet cause.

After dealing with the offending pan of burnt scones, I responded to Carter's text. I let him know that I definitely still wanted to have dinner with him the next night, and would be looking forward to seeing him. He agreed he would pick me up at seven, and I promised to be ready.

I made sure to have his gift-wrapped and set it by the front door so I wouldn't forget to give it to him. The rest of the night was spent putting the finishing touches on my holiday decorations, all the gifts I wanted to give, and cleaning up the mess that Kate had made of the tree once again.

Leaving all of the important ornaments wrapped in their bin had been a smart move on my part. She had even managed to shatter a couple of the hard plastic ones that I had thought would be safe. Shows how much I knew, doesn't it? Luckily they didn't have any sentimental value and it didn't break my heart to throw them in the garbage.

Heading back towards my room for the night I made sure to pick her up and carry her with me. I had moved a small litter box into my bathroom and begun closing my bedroom door at night so she couldn't escape and wreak havoc on any more decorations.

As I got ready for my date the next night, I

pondered how the evening would go. I didn't want to fight with Carter, but I also didn't want to have to lie to him about what my plans were for Christmas Eve. I kind of hoped he wouldn't ask, but I knew that there was a good chance he would want to know. I had a feeling that this date was going to be a make-it-or-break-it at this point of our relationship.

I was absolutely not going to give up my chance to spend Christmas Eve with Brandon's family, and I refused to feel guilty about it. I'd never before dated anyone so insecure and jealous as Carter, and I wasn't sure I was cut out for it.

In spite of my trepidation about the night, dinner went beautifully. It wasn't until we got back to my place afterwards, that things started to get a little sketchy.

We had agreed earlier in the evening to exchange gifts when we got back to my place since we were going to a restaurant for dinner. I wound up getting Carter a sweatshirt and a jersey from his favorite football team. That had been the best I could come up with.

I wrapped them both separately and tied them together with a coordinating ribbon. The package looked pretty if I did say so myself. I handed them to him as he handed me a red gift bag. I wanted to watch him open his gift before opening, so I set it in my lap to wait. He took a long look at me, furrowed his brow and then went ahead and opened his gift.

"Wow, Jenna. This is really nice. Thank you so much, I don't have this jersey yet. Open your gift now, I want to see what you think of it."

"I'm glad you like it, Carter."

I opened the bag and pulled out the tissue paper inside. The paper hid a tiny white box. Opening it up I found two small charms. One was a small kitten. The other was a tiny cocktail glass, reminiscent of the drink he had made me the night we met.

"Do you like them, Jenna? I noticed you always wear a charm bracelet and you had room for more."

"I absolutely love them, thank you so much. I'm going to put them on right now."

"Where did you get the bracelet, does it mean something special to you?"

I paused, closing my fist around the charms. Uh-oh. Here we go, this was the moment of truth. I wasn't going to lie to him about where I got the bracelet, and we were about to see whether or not he could handle it.

"The bracelet was a birthday gift from Brandon."

Watching his face carefully I sat quietly and waited for him to digest the information. At first, he didn't say a word. I could see him very carefully trying to school his features into a neutral expression. Finally, he gave up.

"Jenna, that's it. I'm sorry. I just can't do this. Now you're accepting jewelry from another man? I have put up with a lot when it comes to your relationship with Brandon, but I can't do it anymore. You need to make a decision. You can be friends with him, or you can date me. It's not personal, but I am not cut out to have a girlfriend who has another man in her life."

I looked at him sadly. I supposed I had known this was coming.

"I'm so sorry this is the way it had to end Carter. I've explained to you more times than I can count, Brandon is nothing but a friend. He was married to my best friend and I will not cut him out of my life just because someone I am dating can't stand that I have another male friend. If you think it over and decide that maybe you can let it go, give me a call. My number won't change and I'll still be here."

He looked at me sadly. He left his gift on the arm of

the couch and walked towards the front door.

"Carter. Take your gifts with you, please. I bought them for you, and I still want you to have them. I don't know what else I would do with them."

"Why don't you give them to Brandon?" he asked snidely. "I don't want them. You can do whatever you choose with them. Goodbye, Jenna, I hope you have a very Merry Christmas."

"Goodbye Carter, I'm sorry it ended this way. I hope you have a Merry Christmas too."

I didn't get a response from him, only heard the front door slam. I sat in shock on the couch for a few minutes. In spite of the fact that I had seen this coming from a mile away, I hadn't really expected it to happen tonight. Here we were almost at Christmas, and he was breaking up with me because I had a friend that he couldn't get over his jealousy of.

I looked at the sweater and jersey he left sitting on the arm of the sofa and sighed. What a mess. At least I figured I had the receipt and I could still return them. Brandon wasn't much of a football fan or I would have asked him if he wanted them.

The two charms he had given me as my gift were

still clutched in my hand. I couldn't decide if I wanted to add them to the bracelet, or just put them in my jewelry box for later. They were cute, and I liked them a lot, but I didn't know if I wanted the reminder of his attitude right that second.

Deciding that they belonged in the jewelry box, for now, I carried them back to my room and slipped them into one of the drawers. They would still be there if I decided I wanted to get them out later. Maybe I could mail them to him if I decided I didn't want them.

To my surprise, there weren't a whole lot of emotions rolling around inside me right that moment. I hadn't yet claimed to be in love with Carter, but I had liked him. I enjoyed his company, and I think if he could have gotten over his jealousy of Brandon, we might have been able to build a relationship.

Shrugging to myself, I decided it wasn't worth any tears.

Chapter Nineteen

Friday night and Saturday passed in a whirlwind of nothingness. Sunday morning, I got up and got ready to go see Cassie's parents. I locked Kate in my bathroom with her litter box to protect the tree and set out on my way.

I pulled into their driveway and stopped for a moment looking at all the decorations. This was their first Christmas without their daughter, and yet they had still gone all out decorating just the way she would have wanted. Cassie's favorite holiday was Christmas, and she never accepted any excuses as to why the decorating couldn't be done.

Her mom, Sharon, had the door open before I made it halfway up the walk. As soon as I got to the top of the steps she enveloped me in a big hug.

"Jenna! It's so good to see you my dear. How have you been?

"Hi Sharon! I've missed you. And I've been fine. It's so good to see you. How is Steve?"

She stepped back pushing the door open wide. "Come in child, come in. Steve is absolutely fine. He's getting better every day."

"That's good to hear."

Cassie's dad had taken her death the hardest. She'd been his only daughter and they had been close for her entire life. He was devastated when she got her diagnosis, and after she passed his health had not been the best. I truly feared that he might die from a broken heart.

For a while, it had been touch and go, and I called to check in on him every day. Sharon had been so strong, not only losing her daughter but on the verge of losing her husband as well. Both of Cassie's brothers had stepped up to the plate and done whatever they could for their parents.

"Merry Christmas, Steve," I called out as we passed him sitting in his recliner in the living room.

"Jenna. It's so good to see you. Merry Christmas to you too." Steve got up out of his recliner and came over to give me a big hug. "Thank you so much for coming by, it means so much to us for you to give us your time. We love it when you visit."

I hugged him back, smiling so hard my cheeks hurt. He did indeed look better. "You know I always love to come and see you guys, Steve. I don't know what I would do without you."

We spent the next couple of hours exchanging gifts and eating pastries. Sharon always knew when to go down to Francesca's and get a box, for every holiday and special occasion that purple box had had a prominent presence in our lives.

It filled my heart and soothed my soul to spend time with Cassie's family. In some way, it helped to know that there were other people who knew the pain I was feeling, and who understood my love. I may not miss her as much as her parents did, but I did know our pain had a lot in common.

Before I left, I had to gently ask her mom if she had talked to Evan. Sharon just sighed.

"Don't you worry about him. His grief gets the better of him sometimes."

"I just don't want you guys to think badly of me."

"Jenna. After all these years, really? And I'm going to let you in on a little secret. Before she died, Cassie told me the best thing ever would be for you and Brandon to be together. That nobody would understand the two of you like each other. We would be more than thrilled for the two of you to find happiness. Pay Evan no mind. None at all."

I sighed in relief, reaching over to give her a hug. "Thank you. That means so much to me."

"We love you. Now let's eat."

Right after lunch, I headed back to my place to get ready for Christmas Eve with Brandon's family. I gathered gifts and food and got dressed in my festive best. Brandon texted me about one and let me know that he would pick me up around two if that was okay with me.

Absolutely! I'll be ready.

I sent him my response and carried on with getting ready. I sent my mom and dad a Merry Christmas Eve text and let them know I'd see them bright and early in the morning. I already told them in a phone call earlier in the week that I wouldn't be spending the night tonight. Luckily they understood. I hadn't wanted to hurt their feelings and I felt so blessed that they hadn't given me a hard time.

I made Kate a special Christmas Eve dinner to put in her bowl since I was locking her in the bathroom once more to avoid any mess when I returned. The last thing I wanted was to come home on Christmas Eve and see my tree destroyed. Mischievous little kitty.

Brandon knocked on the door precisely at two. Punctuality had always been one of his strong suits.

"Merry Christmas, are you ready to go?" he asked.

"Absolutely. Would you just give me a hand carrying all of this out to the truck please?"

I handed him the bag of gifts, then grabbed my purse and the casserole off the counter. I had also picked up a box of Francesca's sweets to take with us, even though I knew Amanda or his mother Ruth would be making a dessert. I figured it would give us something to snack on during the afternoon.

We took our time driving to Amanda's place, as the roads turned slippery with the cold. I loved a white Christmas and secretly hoped that it would snow overnight.

As we pulled up to his sister's house his Mother's car was already in the driveway. All of the outside lights were on, as well as the porch light, and their house looked like a Christmas Wonderland. All it was missing was the snow.

Liam answered the door to let us in and we immediately heard the Christmas music playing somewhere in the background. He smiled, giving us both hugs.

"Merry Christmas, you two! " he opened the door wide. "Come on in, before Amanda starts hollering that we're letting in the cold."

Brandon and I both scooted inside, me turning sideways to get myself and the boxes through the door. Liam relieved me of the boxes from one arm and took them to the kitchen for me. I traded Brandon, giving him the other box and taking the bag of gifts so I could put them under the tree.

Ruth came bustling out from the kitchen, wearing a Christmas apron and covered in flour. She wrapped me up in a big hug, holding me for a long time.

"Jenna, it is so good to see you. We have missed you."

I wrapped my arms around her, hugging her back. "I've missed you too. Merry Christmas."

"Thank you for coming," I heard Amanda call from the other room and I followed her voice into the sun room

She had both twins on her lap, gesturing for me to go ahead and pick one up. "Help yourself," she said.

I reached out and took Cassie from her arm. She had grown so much in the couple of weeks since I'd seen her. Both of them had. I rested her on my hip, swaying back and forth to soothe her.

"You're such a natural with babies, Jenna. I can't wait till you have a couple of your own."

I laughed. "That won't be anytime soon. You have to at least have a boyfriend to get babies."

"What happened to that young man you were dating last time you came by?"

"It just didn't work out. No big deal."

Amanda took the hint that I didn't want to talk about it and let the subject drop. "Well,l at least you know you can come and borrow babies from me anytime you want."

Christmas Eve with Brandon's family was full of all the things a Christmas Eve should be. There was laughter and love. We ate good food and opened presents. I enjoyed it more than I had enjoyed a Christmas Eve in a very long time.

As it got late, I helped Amanda to put the twins to bed. We took a minute to have a whispered conversation just outside their door.

"So..." she looked at me slyly. "You and Brandon are spending an awful lot of time together lately, aren't you?"

I looked at her sideways. "We see each other about once a week. Sometimes a little bit more."

"I know I'm a nosy busybody but are the two of you getting close?" She winked at me.

I giggled. "Probably not in the way you seem to be insinuating."

"You know, Cassie told me that she would like nothing more than for the two of you to get together. She felt like having the two people she loves most love each other would be amazing."

I let out a big sigh. "You know she's actually written us both letters, where she certainly insinuated that she thought we should begin dating. But I was dating Carter right up until Friday night, and I highly doubt Brandon is ready for another relationship. We talked about it briefly and both agree that right now we are just doing what we are comfortable with, and we'll see what the future holds when it arrives."

"Well, I, for one, am glad the two of you aren't ruling it out. I loved Cassie, but Brandon is my brother. I want him to be happy, and I think that you would be able to make him that. The two of you make a very striking couple."

"Thank you for your blessing, Amanda. I appreciate that you guys care for me enough that you would allow me into your family, and that you're actually encouraging me to take up with your brother. I love you guys like family, whether or not Brandon and I ever get together."

She grinned and wrapped me in a great big hug. "That's good to hear. We've become attached to you, and we won't be giving you up anytime soon."

We returned to the group sitting in the sun room, and settled onto the couch. Before we knew it the night had gone by, and the clock was striking midnight.

Brandon looked at me and raised his eyebrows, and I nodded. It was time for me to be headed home. We both stood, and began saying our goodbyes. After lots of hugs and merry Christmases, we headed out the front door.

He drove me back to my place slowly, and just as we were pulling into the drive the first white flakes began to fall from the sky. For a moment I just sat looking at out it. We were going to wake up to a white Christmas tomorrow, I just knew it.

I turned to look at him. "Do you want to come in for a few minutes? I know it's late, and you don't have to."

"Sure. I don't have anywhere else to be."

I let us in the front door and headed back to release Kate from her confinement. As I did that he turned on the Christmas lights and the tree. I made us both hot cocoa and we settled onto the couch, leaving the TV off and the Christmas music on.

Throughout the course of our half-hour conversation, I had to chase Kate out of the tree twice.

"She's quite persistent isn't she?"

"Oh, you have no idea. She takes after her namesake in a way I had never imagined would be possible. Had I know she would adopt some of Cassie's more tenacious qualities, I might have named her something lazy, like Bertha."

Brandon snorted with laughter. "Bertha? That's just mean."

"Well. It would have made my life a little less hectic."

He drained the last of his cocoa and set the cup on the coffee table. "Thanks for coming tonight. We all loved having you with us."

"Thanks for inviting me. You guys really took the sting out of the holiday for me."

We each sat lost in our own thoughts for the next few minutes. I looked over at him and watched the emotions play across his face.

"Brandon? Do you want to stay? We don't have to get up alone on Christmas morning. You can use the hide-a-bed or even sleep with me. The bed's a king, and

I promise to stay on my own side."

He looked momentarily astounded and I feared I crossed a line. Before I could take it back he looked over and smiled.

"You know, if I didn't have to get home and let Toby out, I would take you up on it. But he can't stay indoors by himself for that long."

"Ah, I didn't even think of Toby, the poor guy. He's probably already more than anxious for you to get home."

I stood to take our cups to the kitchen sink. Brandon caught me in a hug as I came back out.

"Thank you for the invitation. It would have made a nice Christmas morning."

I backed away and stared up at him. "You're always welcome."

We stood like that for an eternity, just gazing into each other's eyes. He leaned down, for a brief second I panicked that he might kiss me. And he did, but just a chaste kiss on the forehead.

"Merry Christmas Jenna."

"Merry Christmas Brandon. Drive safe okay? The snow is really starting to come down out there. Text me when you get home so I know you made it?"

He agreed and slipped out the door. I watched him pick his way the sidewalk, stepping carefully on the slick surface. He climbed into the truck, started it up and pulled away.

"It looks like it's just you and me now, Kate."

We retired to my room, where I elected to soak in the tub while I waited for Brandon to send me the all safe text. I had reached the edge of worry when it finally came through.

Roads were slick, but I am home safe and sound. Merry Christmas.

I sighed with relief as I responded. Then I realized that if the roads got too bad overnight I might not make it to my parents for Christmas morning. Deciding not to borrow trouble from tomorrow, I got out and dried off. Kate had already curled up on her pillow and began to purr as I climbed in next to her.

"Merry first Christmas, Katey Cat."

Chapter Twenty

For the first time in years, I slept in on Christmas morning. Even Kate didn't wake me for her breakfast. It was after seven before I actually got up, showered and put on my holiday onesie pajamas.

I grabbed the two bags of gifts for my family and the one of food and for the first time peeked out the front window. A blanket of white covered the ground. I loved the idea of staring at it, but the idea of driving to my parents in it was a whole other story. They only lived about 20 minutes down the road, but with this weather, it might take me an hour to get there. Just as I was trying to decide whether to brave it, my phone rang. It was my dad on the other end.

"Hello honey. Good morning and Merry Christmas. I saw the snow outside. Do you want me to come and get you?"

"Thanks Dad! You're the best. I would appreciate it. I was starting to wonder whether I would make it with the snow. My car is good but I don't know how slippery it is."

"I'm bringing the truck, and I'll see you in about twenty minutes."

Ever so thankful that my dad was always there for me, to do anything I might need, I sat on the couch and waited for him to arrive. He showed up right on time, leading me to believe the roads might not be as bad as I had expected.

"You sure you won't mind bringing me home later Daddy?" I asked him.

"Of course not sugar. Do I ever mind?"

I laughed and shook my head. He never did mind, no matter what I asked. My mom had breakfast going when we got back to the house, and my sister was already there as well. She must have spent the night before because she was not an early riser.

We spent the day together, just the four of us, enjoying family-type things on Christmas Day. I had brought a box of Francesca's sweets that we nibbled on throughout the day. We opened presents, watched Christmas movies and generally enjoyed each other's company.

I texted Brandon about 10 am, just to say Merry Christmas. He texted me back and let me know that if I got bored later that night he planned to be home too, and maybe we could get together. I told him I'd let him know when I was on my way back to my place..

We always had Christmas dinner early, then spent the rest of the afternoon snacking. My mom roasted a turkey with all the trimmings. It was exactly what a holiday was supposed to be. In spite of missing Cassie, I had an excellent day.

It started to snow again right before we began to eat, and I worried about getting home. My dad didn't mind driving in the snow, but if the weather got really bad I didn't want to have to worry about him getting home.

I texted Brandon, and let him know that I was going to be home fairly early because I didn't want my dad out driving in the snow. Instead of telling me he'd meet me at the house, he offered to come pick me up from my parents. The three of our houses formed a semi-triangle, so it wouldn't be too far out of his way, and then my dad wouldn't have to go out and drive in it.

I asked my mom if she'd mind if he came by for a bit. Of course, her answer was to tell him to get his butt over here. So I sent him a text.

We're just getting ready to eat, so if you want to, come on over and have Christmas dinner with us, and then you can take me home.

Informing me that he'd just been ready to leave his mom and dad's, he said he would be there in a half an hour or so, depending on the weather.

My mom looked at me sideways as we prepared the dishes to set to the table. "So, you and Brandon are spending an awful lot of time together aren't you?"

The millionth person to notice. I sighed.

"Mom. Yes, we are. But don't read anything into it. We've helped each other get through a lot this year."

"I know, I'm just checking. He's a nice man, and I

think you could use one of those. Whatever happened to Carter, anyways?"

"Mom, I don't want to talk about Carter. The short story is he couldn't get over his jealousy of Brandon, and we broke up."

"Well, that's too bad, but apparently he wasn't the one for you."

"That's kind of what I figured."

We just finished setting the table and were getting ready to eat when Brandon knocked on the door. My dad let him in, welcoming him heartily.

Dinner was delicious and we sat around the table for almost an hour and a half, just making small talk and enjoying each other's company. As I looked out the window, I noticed even more snow pouring down.

"It looks like Brandon and I should probably head out guys. That snow is coming down and I don't want to be stuck on the road somewhere trying to get home."

My mom looked out the window. "You guys could both spend the night here if you wanted."

"Thanks mom, but neither of us have the stuff we need for a sleepover. I think we'll make it home just fine if we leave now."

Brandon nodded his agreement. "I promise to drive careful and I'll get her home in one piece. The truck has four-wheel drive."

"We know you will," my dad said. "We trust you. You guys enjoy Christmas night. Text us to let us know you made it safely, okay."

I nodded my agreement and after a fifteen-minute round of hugs, merry Christmases and drive safes, we got in the truck. I asked Brandon if he wanted to come over and just plan to stay. That way neither of us had to be alone for the rest of Christmas.

"If we can swing by my place and pick up Toby, I'd love to."

I laughed at him. "Of course you can bring Toby. Let's go get him."

What should have been a twenty-minute drive to my place turned into an hour-long round trip as we swung by Brandon's for him to pick up some things and grab Toby. The snow was still coming down as we left his place. By the time we reached my condo, there was a good three to four inches on the ground. We all rushed inside from the driveway, covered in snow by the time we got to the front door. Toby was having a blast.

All three of us squished in the front door at once, leaving a puddle as the snow melted off of our clothes and Toby's fur. I laughed, kicked off my boots and headed to the bathroom for a towel.

Luckily I'd made it a point to do big grocery shopping earlier in the week. I hit both the regular grocery store and Costco. The cupboards were full, the fridge was stocked, and there wasn't a whole lot we should need if we couldn't leave the house anytime soon. I dug Toby's dishes out of the pantry and filled them.

With hot cocoa in the crock pot and Francesca's pastries on the counter, we headed to the living room to watch Christmas movies.

A couple hours later as we sat eating the leftovers my mom had sent home with us, Brandon looked at me with serious eyes.

"Thanks for inviting me. My family wanted me to stay, but I wasn't quite in the mood for that sort of visit. I really didn't want to be alone either, though."

"No thanks needed. I was kind of in the same boat. Not quite wanting to be around the hustle and bustle of family, but not wanting to be alone either. It's a strange place to be."

We were quiet for a little while longer as the movie played unnoticed in the background.

Brandon turned to me again. "It's only been eight months; do you think it's terrible of me that I am trying to learn to live again? I'm not forgetting her. I just don't want to be miserable all the time."

"Brandon, are you serious? You know if Cassie had her way neither one of us would have been sad for a single minute. She wanted nothing more for us than to be happy. I think she would be thrilled to know that you were trying to stop grieving. We'll always miss her. Always. But that doesn't mean we have to spend the rest of our lives being sad. I've been trying to take the steps to live my life as well, not dwelling on what we lost but, rejoicing in what we had. I had an amazing best friend for almost my whole life."

"I know, I know. It just seems wrong; she was my wife. I feel like I am somehow dishonoring her memory by moving on."

"Just keep in mind that that's what she would have wanted. Every time I want to wallow in my grief, I remind myself that if she were here, she'd slap me upside the head for it. We both know it."

I got a half-smile out of him for that. "I know you're right, it's just such a strange thing to be coping with. I've never had anyone die on me before, it sucks that my first had to be my wife."

"You're right, the whole situation sucked. And at the risk of sounding cliche, I also try to remind myself that she's no longer in pain. She wouldn't have wanted to live that way, and she made sure we knew it. I like to think of her now as looking down on us, encouraging us, and watching to see how things go."

He chuckled. "And trying to influence things as best she can from wherever she is?"

"Well, can you blame her? She's always been persistent, why on Earth should death get in the way of that?"

"You do have a solid point."

"Did you get a Christmas card from her?" Brandon looked down at his hands as he asked.

I nodded. "Showed up in the regular old mail the other day. Complete with a handwritten letter, of course. I assume you got one too?"

He nodded, a small smile on his face. Neither of us shared the contents of our cards, but somehow we knew that what she had written in one was probably very similar to what she had written in the other.

Somehow, hours passed, and we found ourselves nearing midnight. I looked at the clock in surprise.

"Where did the time go? Are you about ready for bed?"

"I could sleep."

"We have the same choices as the other night when I offered to let you stay. I can sleep here on the couch and you can have my bed. or we can sleep together in my bed and I promise to stay on my own side. I wouldn't make you sleep on the couch; I think it might be shorter than you are."

"I don't mind sharing the space with you, I'm not afraid of little ol' you," he teased me.

"Well, maybe you should be." I raised my eyebrows at him in jest.

We laughed together, each of us heading to separate bathrooms to get ready for bed. As we got back to my room I saw Kate, already asleep on her pillow.

"Oh, I forgot. You might have to jostle with Kate for your side of the bed. She's kind of claimed it for herself, and nobody else has ever slept over there."

"I'm pretty sure Kate and I can come to an understanding."

We climbed into bed, Brandon took Kate's pillow and putting it between us, using one of the spare ones that I had for himself. She opened one eye and looked at him, yawned and promptly curled around to face her butt towards him.

"Well, I guess that settles that. Luckily for you, she doesn't usually pass gas."

He chuckled." Well, if she starts getting stinky I will simply turn the pillow around, and face her your direction."

We shut the lights off and I heard him say I deeply. "Goodnight Jenna. Thanks again for having me."

"Goodnight Brandon. I'm really glad you came."

I slept peacefully the entire night through. Waking up the next morning I was disoriented at first, finding myself tangled not only in my comforter but in Brandon's arms. Somehow, as we slept, the two of us had managed to commingle.

And the sound of his deep breathing Brandon was not yet awake. I couldn't decide whether to quietly slip out of his arms and out of bed or to just lie there still until he woke up. Would he be embarrassed to find us together this way? I knew not to read anything into it, sometimes when you're sleeping your body does strange things.

Before I had a chance to make up my mind I felt him stir. He lay still for a moment, barely breathing. He did not immediately pull away from me, which left me with the decision of whether or not to be the one to make the first move. In the moment, I decided to just lay there and wait to see his reaction.

He slowly removed his arm from on top of y waist, stopping as he attempted to pull the other arm out from under me, but obviously not wanting to wake me.

"You can have your arm back, I'm awake."

He stilled, then gently removed it. "I'm sorry."

"Don't be sorry. It's not a big deal."

I rolled over to on my opposite side so I would be able to see his face better. His expression held a mixture of wonder and discomfort.

"In case it matters, I slept better last night than I have in months."

"Good. I'm glad. If there is any night of the year we deserve to have good sleep, Christmas is it."

He rolled onto his back, placing his hands behind his head. Toby whined from outside my door, and I got up to let him in but returned to my spot beneath the comforter to escape the chill in the house.

Thankful for the Nest app I grabbed my phone off the night table so I could turn up the heat and start the coffee.

"We should have coffee momentarily."

"That makes you my favorite human on Earth right now."

Chapter Twenty-One

Brandon went home after breakfast, his mood somewhat somber. I didn't quite know what to make of it but I didn't want to push him. He waved goodbye as he walked out the front door, promising to call me later in the week.

I spent the rest of the day denying to myself how good it felt to wake up in his arms. Guilt swamped me. Even though I knew Cassie said she would be just fine with us getting together, I couldn't shake the sense that I shouldn't be sleeping with my best friend's husband, even if all we did was sleep.

It hadn't crossed my mind at any point that we would wind up in tangled in each other's arms the next morning. I really thought we would spend the night sleeping peacefully on our own sides of the bed.

Between Christmas and New Year's was always a little bit of a twilight zone for me. There was no work, and also not much else going on.

When I didn't hear from Brandon for the first couple days, I imagined him grappling with his own guilt. As the New Year drew closer I reflected on the fact that it would be our first full year without Cassie.

New Year's Eve was another one of those holidays we had always celebrated together. As much as I enjoyed it, I was looking forward to getting through the last of these firsts without her. The first one was always the hardest, and I knew the others would get easier in the years to come.

Brandon finally texted me on Thursday.

New Year's Eve party at Amanda and Liam's. Do you want to come?

I didn't reply right away. My parents had invited me to come to their place, and my sister Kendall had invited me over for movie watching also. I had to admit, spending time with Amanda and Liam and the twins sounded like a much better time.

Absolutely. What can I bring?

Just yourself... Would it be wrong to tell you I miss you?

Nope, in fact, it would be great... Because I've missed you too

Biting my inner cheek as I hit the send button, I couldn't help but smile. Being giddy like a schoolgirl over his admission of missing me, almost drowned out the guilt I felt for flirting with my best friend's husband.

I'll pick you up at 6. Have a good day.

I spent some time pacing the kitchen floor, unsure of what I should make of my innermost feelings. Kate chased my untied shoe for a moment, then gave up when I accidentally kicked her into the table leg.

"I'm so sorry kitty. I didn't mean to."

She gave me a disgruntled look and stomped off to the other room. I just giggled at her. Cats were such funny creatures.

Before I knew it New Year's Eve had rolled around.

I took extra care with my appearance while trying

to not make it look like I had tried too hard. My favorite jewelry complimented my outfit and I pulled my hair up in a "messy" bun, leaving soft curls around my face and neck. I looked in the mirror, pleased with my appearance and complimenting myself on my makeup skills, then went to the kitchen to gather my offering for the party.

I'd gone to Francesca's and asked her to make a pastry spread fit for celebrating the new year, and she hadn't disappointed me. Even though Brandon had told me there would only be two other couples besides Amanda and Liam the pastries filled three large bakery boxes. Everybody would be having leftovers for days!

I yelled for Brandon to come in as he knocked, while I settled the purple boxes back into the bags Francesca had sent for me to carry them in.

"Wow. You look stunning." He seemed shocked.

I gave him a nervous smile. "Thank you. You look great too."

He spent another minute studying me. I stood still, letting him look. Finally, he shifted his attention to the bag.

"What's this?"

"Francesca's of course. I haven't had a New Year's

Eve without her baking since the year she opened."

He nodded. "Of course. Are you ready to go?"

"Let's do it."

The snow of Christmas had mostly melted, leaving only a few white patches long the sides of the road. Toby, riding in the back seat, had his head out the window taking in the cool air. Brandon had brought him along to hang out in the basement since he did not do well with fireworks and loud noises when he got left home alone.

"Are you cold? I have another jacket back there." He started to reach his arm around to grab it.

"I'm fine, don't worry about it. We're almost there."

We made it to his sister's house before any of the other guests, and let Toby run on in while we carried our stuff up the walk. Amanda met us at the door.

"I told you not to bring anything! We have so much food." Amanda laughed as she eyes the bag on my arm.

"But do you have Francesca's pastries?"

She shook her head.

"Then you do not have everything you need for a perfect New Year's Eve."

"Okay, I get it. Let's get them to the buffet table and

we'll find a space for them."

The other couples arrived and introductions were made. We sat around visiting until dinner when I helped Amanda remove the lids from the warmers and expose the delicious buffet. They had ordered instead of cooking it themselves to make the evening more relaxing, and everything looked and smelled wonderful.

We almost made it through the meal before the twins started fussing. Brandon and I both waved at Amanda to finish her last few bites so we could pick them up. He grabbed Cassie and I grabbed Connor. Both of us working to soothe them so their mama could finish her meal.

We took them back to the nursery and changed them before returning to the dining room. Amanda settled herself in to feed them and we went to help clean up the kitchen.

"You two sure make a good team!" she called out after us.

Brandon caught my eye and winked. We did indeed make a good team.

Midnight crept up on us in the midst of our laughter and camaraderie. At some point, Liam had turned on the music and we danced. The last song before midnight was a slow love song. Brandon grabbed my hand and tugged me close. My eyes met his and we spent long seconds searching each other as if looking for the answer to the world's most important questions in each other's soul.

Leaning in close, I settled my head on his chest as his arms tightened around me. I could hear his heartbeat as I pressed against him. We stayed that way for the rest of the dance. As the song ended we had about three minutes until midnight.

"Want to go out to the deck to watch the fireworks?"

At my nod, he went to the closet and grabbed our jackets and a spare blanket. We slipped out the back door, sliding it closed behind us. We found our space against the railing and bundled together in the blanket.

"Can you believe this year is coming to an end?" So much of it had passed in a blur, I barely remembered many of the individual days.

"In a way, it seems like it lasted forever, and yet flew by all too fast at the same time," he agreed, his voice barely more than a whisper.

"It had some amazing highs and terrible lows. Life as a human is such a roller coaster."

"I agree. And in spite of the both beautiful and painful start to the year, I think it is ending on a fairly good note, don't you?"

My voice caught in my throat and the best answer I could give him meant just nodding my head, which caused him to smile. We could hear the others indoors begin counting down to midnight, as we met each other's gaze.

My emotions felt like a runaway train. How dare I feel like this about my best friend's husband? But she gave us her blessing. Never before had I had so many thoughts in the space of six seconds.

Brandon's hand had moved up to cup the back of my head. I tilted slightly back, bunching his shirt in my hands. Everything that passed between us during those seconds did so in absolute silence. My last thought before our lips met was to hope Cassie really would be happy for us.

The fireworks began before we parted. The kiss was long and slow, and even through my closed eyes, I could see the flashes of light going on around us. I heard the neighborhood cheering and exclaiming "happy new year!" As we separated I opened my eyes, meeting his gaze. The first thing I saw besides him? A firework burst across the sky, filling it with pink and silver light in the shape of a heart. I knew right then that Cassie used that moment to signal her blessing.

"Happy new year," he whispered.

"Happy new year."

We stood quietly on the deck, wrapped in a blanket, and watched the rest of the fireworks before going back inside. When we got back in the house Amanda hugged us both, handing us a glass of champagne.

"Happy new year you two!"

We toasted and had some more of Francesca's splendid pastries. Amanda offered me more champagne and I began to decline, but Brandon interrupted.

"Go ahead. I'm driving, you're not."

Amanda giggled with glee as she topped off my glass. "This is the only night I'll be able to drink for a while since I pumped and don't have to worry about nursing the twins. Join me!"

Of course, I couldn't deny her. We enjoyed more dancing, and more champagne, us ladies making the most of our evening. About an hour later I had about reached the end of my endurance for the night. I sank into the couch, leaning my head back.

Brandon's voice next to my ear startled me. "Are you ready to head home?"

I jumped. "Oh. Sure. Ready when you are."

We gathered our things and said our goodbyes. I must have dozed off in the truck on the way home because before I knew it Brandon had opened my door to help me out. The walk had turned slippery with the falling temperatures, and I struggled to keep my balance thanks to the heels on my boots. Brandon wrapped his arm around my waist to hold me up.

"Thanks. I should have just slipped them off and ran in barefoot."

"Ha. No need to get frostbite on your toes when I can help you up to the door."

We made it inside without incident, Brandon escorting me all the way to the couch. Toby immediately began looking for Kate, who had hightailed it out of there as soon as she realized he was with us.

Reaching down to unzip my boots, I glanced sideways at Brandon. "Thanks so much for inviting me tonight. I had the most amazing time." I very carefully made no mention of our time on the deck.

"It wouldn't have been the same without you. Thanks for coming."

"Want some coffee or a pastry?" Amanda had sent most of the leftovers from Francesca's home with me and I had no idea how I could eat them all before they went bad.

I stood to head into the kitchen, but all the champagne must have gone to my head because I stumbled, and just barely caught myself on the arm of the couch. Brandon jumped up to help me as I giggled.

"Maybe we should just get you to bed instead."

"I'm not as drunk as I look, I promise."

He shook his head, trying to hold back his laughter. "Maybe not, but it is awfully late."

"Coffee helps. And Francesca's pastries make everything better... Almost." My mood soured for a moment, thinking of the main thing they could never make better. They couldn't bring Cassie back.

Brandon just smiled. "I'd better be getting home."

The silence stretched between us for a moment, neither of us saying a word. Our eyes met, and I sighed.

"You don't *have* to go home. Do you want to stay again?"

I held my breath as I waited for his response. He seemed to be holding his as he tried to make up his mind. Finally, he shook his head.

"I'd better get back to the house. Thanks for asking though."

Disappointment reared its ugly head, but in spite of the alcohol I managed to not try and convince him to stay, even though I wanted to. He probably needed time to process his feelings, which, if I was honest with myself, I needed too.

"Okay. Drive carefully and text me that you got home safe, so I don't worry. The roads are icy."

He raised his eyebrows. "How would you know? You slept all the way here."

"Shush. Just do it, or I'll hide your keys and you'll have to stay here."

After we both laughed he got a serious look on his face. "You turned this New Year's Eve into something special when I was scared it would be painfully suffocating. Thank you."

I reached out and laid a hand on his arm, leaning

towards him. "I feel the same way. Had I spent it anywhere else, with anyone else, it would have been terrible." I gave his arm a gentle squeeze and let go.

With a smile he headed out the front door, leaving me alone with my champagne laden thoughts to go to sleep alone for the first time in the new year.

Chapter Twenty-Two

The first day of the New Year greeted me with a champagne headache. Tylenol and a warm shower where the first order of business to try to get rid of it. I debated texting Brandon, wondering if it was too forward of me to have invited him to stay last night. Our kiss at the stroke of midnight had seared itself into my memory.

That day my emotions were torn. My brain and heart warred, guilt and excitement pitting themselves against each other. On the one hand, I could not believe

I'd kissed my best friend's husband. On the other, however, I was excited for the possibility of what was yet to come.

Before Cassie passed away I never looked at Brandon as anything other than practically my brother-in-law. It went without saying that if Cassie were still alive, Brandon I would have never been anything more. But she was gone, and we were here.

Even looking at her handwritten note, the one telling us she hoped we got together someday, I couldn't bring myself to accept that what I was doing was okay. I knew she would want him to move forward with his life. She had told us so. In spite of her written reassurances, I still struggled with the concept.

When I got out of the shower I had a surprise text from Carter. It said nothing more than happy New Year. I chose not to answer him.

I busied myself with work. I had over a week's worth to catch up on, which meant there was plenty to keep me occupied. The week flew by in a flash and I found myself on Saturday morning before I knew it. The entire week had passed with no contact from Brandon. Carter had sent two more texts, both of which I deleted.

Brandon had a birthday coming up at the end of the month and I struggled to pick out a birthday gift for him. I wanted to choose something meaningful, like the bracelet he'd gotten for me. Unfortunately, the ideas were scarce. I thought maybe a day at the mall would help.

Turns out it didn't help at all. I browsed for hours in just about every store the mall held and left with hands just as empty as when I arrived. I saw nobody that I knew and moved through the day as if in a bubble.

Leaving the parking lot, I took a left turn instead of the right that would have taken me home, intent on going for a drive to clear my head. I followed the interstate and wound down around the lakefront, looking out at the frothing water. The wind had picked up and white caps were forming on the waves. I pulled into a parking spot facing the water and just sat, letting my thoughts wander where they wanted.

As the sun went down I headed back toward home, grabbing something to eat on the way. Still no word from Brandon, and I decided that I needed to give him his space. He knew where to find me.

Sunday came and went, and for the first time in

months, we didn't do our usual Sunday brunch. The space I thought I should give him stretched into days. I missed him and I missed Toby fiercely.

The week before his birthday Amanda called me.

"Hey Jenna! Long time, no see. I was starting to wonder if you had been abducted by aliens."

"No, I'm still here. What's up?"

"Well, a certain brother of mine has a birthday coming up and we want to throw him a little surprise party. Just dinner on Saturday night, nothing extravagant or anything. We'd love for you to come."

"Oh... well..." I didn't know what to say. He hadn't made any attempt to contact me and I would hate to ruin his birthday party by showing up there if he didn't want to see me.

"I know he hasn't called you. But he misses you. He is just dealing with guilt. I think he'd be thrilled if you were there."

"I don't know..."

"Please? I miss you and you have to see how fast the twins are growing!"

"Playing hardball are you? I can always come over and see the twins on a night that you aren't having a party."

"You right, you can. You are welcome to come by whenever you want. But I'd really like you to come to the party, and I know Brandon would too."

"Can I think about it?"

"Of course. I'm not going to force you. Are you busy tonight? Want to come by for dinner and see the twins? I'd love to see you and Liam is gone for a business meeting until tomorrow night."

"That I can do. Want me to grab takeout on my way over?"

"We can just order when you get here. Then you don't have to make an extra stop."

"Perfect. I'll see you in a bit."

The night I spent hanging out with Amanda and the twins lifted my spirits. Of course, she managed to convince me to come to the dinner while I was there, but I knew she would. It didn't take much since I knew I wanted to attend. I just hoped he'd be as happy to see me as she thought he would.

The week passed interminably slowly. Saturday rolled around and I found myself looking for things to do to pass the time. I made the mistake of getting ready way too early and then having nothing to do until it was time to go. I finally ended up sending Amanda a text, asking her if I could come early.

Her response was "of course," followed by a number of exclamation points. Checking whether she needed me to pick anything up on the way, I grabbed my purse and headed out the door.

As I pulled into the drive the garage door rolled up and I saw Liam inside waving me in.

"We just want to keep as much room as possible in the driveway," he said as I got out. He shut the garage door behind me.

"I thought Amanda said not many people were coming."

"Okay, you got me. Amanda wanted your presence to be a surprise. So she asked me to hide your car." Liam shrugged. "I do as I'm told. Nothing more, nothing less."

I laughed. It was so like Amanda to play the game. Following him into the house I set Brandon's gift on the table that Amanda indicated.

I spent the next hour and a half attempting to help Amanda set up before the guests began arriving. Their mom and dad were the first, both of them hugging me.

Three more cars pulled into the drive before Amanda announced we were just waiting on Brandon to show up. She introduced me to their cousin and his wife, a couple of Brandon's college buddies and an aunt and uncle. We all sat around chatting until Liam announced Brandon had just pulled into the driveway.

I took a spot near the back of the crowd so my presence wouldn't be immediately obvious. Amanda stood next to me, grinning from ear to ear. Each of us had a baby in one arm.

Brandon's smile was genuine as Liam let him in the front door. He looked quite surprised to see the small crowd welcoming him.

"Happy birthday!" everyone called out. "Surprise!"

He made his way through the crowd saying hellos. Just before he got to me Amanda took the baby and made herself scarce with a wink. As our eyes met he looked briefly startled by my presence.

"I can leave, if you would prefer," I whispered softly, so the others wouldn't hear us.

"No. Please stay. I'm glad you're here, really. I'm sorry I've been so quiet lately."

"You don't have to apologize. I understand."

We endured a minute of awkward silence. He reached out and touched my hand. I looked down at the physical contact before looking up to meets his eyes once more. His skin was warm, almost searing against my own.

"I've missed you."

"Yeah? You always know where to find me, right? I haven't gone anywhere."

He exhaled deeply. "I know. I've been struggling. But seeing you again just makes it all the more clear. I don't want to go so long without seeing you again. If you'll have me? Brunch tomorrow, like it should be?"

I quirked my lips up in a half-smile. "Well... I suppose if you bring me the best brunch ever, and Toby. I've missed him so much. I almost went over while you were at work so I could play with him."

His eyes lit up. "So you'd make the trip to see the dog, but not me? I see how it is."

"Do you? I at least knew Toby would be happy to see me." I couldn't resist the last little jab at his absence.

"Ouch." He held his hand over his heart. "You wound me so with your words."

"Like you wounded me with your absence?"

"Okay, I give." He raised both hands as if in surrender. "I will never be able to win a war of words with you, so I should just shut up now before I get any farther behind."

I gave him a wink. "It's good that you know your limitations."

"I'm going to be paying for this for a very long time, aren't I?"

"Maybe. Depends on how much you try to make it up to me."

Amanda came over as we were talking. "Sorry to interrupt, but it's time to sit down to dinner and maybe let him spend some time with his other guests?"

"Jeez, Amanda, I suppose." I gave her a grin as we headed for the dining room. Brandon went ahead of us and she elbowed me in the side.

"See. I told you so. Aren't you glad you came?"

"Yes, yes. You were right. I am very glad I came."

Dinner was excellent and the company even more so. Brandon's parents and his aunt and uncle headed home after the food, waving off offers of cake and ice cream.

"Us old folks don't need sugar before bed,"

Brandon's mom teased. "It was so good to see you Jenna, please don't be a stranger."

"I won't, promise. It was good to see you too." I hugged her gently. "And it was nice to meet you," I shook hands with his aunt and uncle.

The six of us that were left served cake and Brandon's buddies told some stories about their college years. I settled back into the couch at his side, listening to tales of his life before we knew each other. I'd been thinking a lot about destiny lately, or fate, whatever you want to call it. How one single decision had a ripple effect on the rest of your life, even if you weren't aware of it at the time.

Imagine if Brandon and Cassie had never met. How different would things be at right that moment? Would she have even been sick? Which things are written into the stars, meaning that they happen no matter what? And which things are purely chance?

I believed strongly that every person who appeared in your life did so for a reason. That reason may never be revealed to you, but perhaps it was a catalyst for something that was meant to be. To guide you, and steer you down the path that the universe wanted you to be on.

"Earth to Jenna? Hello?"

I shook my head as if to dislodge the thoughts that had been floating around in my mental space. "Yes? Did I miss something?"

Everyone in the room laughed. "Only ninety percent of the conversation," Brandon teased.

"Sorry about that. I guess I let my imagination wander away from me."

Finally, I needed to head home. I stood up and thanked everyone for a lovely evening. "I hope I will be able to get my car out of the garage?"

Brandon stood with me. "You sit Liam; I can go let her out. The only car in the drive is mine, so if I'm in the way I can move it over to let her out."

We walked down the stairs to the garage. "She had you hide your car, did she?"

"Yep. Said she wanted my presence to be a surprise. I almost didn't come; you know?"

We stopped next to my car. "I'm really glad you did. And I'm sorry I disappeared on you like that, just after..." His voice trailed off.

"I know. Like I said earlier, I get it. I waged some

pretty heavy internal battles myself. I still am, to be honest."

"I think it will be a regular thing for a while yet. I'm so torn."

"Well, the silver lining to the struggle is that we both know where the other is coming from. Nobody else is going to understand our situation quite like we do."

"You have a point. I guess if you can be patient with me-"

"And you with me," I interrupted him gently.

"We just might make it through this. But there are still a couple of difficult days coming up. Our anniversary, and then the one-year mark of her passing away."

"Well, I'll be here if you need me. You know that."

"Oh, I'll need you alright." He reached out, pulling me into a hug. I gladly accepted, melting into his arms.

"Happy birthday, Brandon."

Chapter Twenty-Three

Winter waned and began to release its icy grip on the world. Weeks passed, day in and day out being much of the same. April arrived and I began to dread Brandon and Cassie's wedding anniversary. I wanted to do something special for him on that day, but I couldn't decide what. I wanted it to be a fond remembrance, and bring on as little pain as possible.

At brunch on Sunday just a few days before their anniversary, Brandon looked over at me with a serious look in his eye. "Would you get together with me on

Thursday and eat the wedding cake?"

"I'd love to. Do you want to plan on having dinner too?"

"That would be nice. I was thinking about taking the day off work, do you think you could get the day too? Maybe we could go do something to keep our minds occupied?"

"Absolutely, one of the perks from working at home is that I can structure my hours however I want. They don't care as long as the work gets done. What do you think you'd like to do?"

He shrugged. "I haven't got the faintest idea. I just know I don't want to sit at home and dwell on it."

"Well we have a couple of days, we can think of something."

Toby whined and jumped up onto the couch between us as if he knew what we were talking about. I pet him gently, snuggling him close to me. Kate jumped up on my other side, settling between my lap and the arm of the sofa. It took a while, but she had come to terms with Toby being in her space. They were even on the verge of becoming friends.

The week leading up to their anniversary was tense.

Guilt reared its ugly head again, leaving me sad that I was the one here to celebrate her first anniversary with her husband and not her.

The day before their anniversary a small white box appeared in my mailbox. The return address was that of Cassie's lawyer. It didn't surprise me at all that she had chosen to send something for this special day.

Taking it inside, I opened it and looked at the contents. There was an envelope with Brandon's name on it and a folded note with my name on the front. It also contained a small box wrapped in a purple ribbon, with a name tag reading 'to my husband.'

Inhaling deeply, I opened the folded note.

Hi Jenna! How are you? We're coming up on the one-year anniversary of Brandon and my wedding, which I know you're aware of. At this point, I hope you two have been spending lots of time together, and will be able to comfort each other. This package came to you, instead of him, because I wanted to be sure he would get it on time. (Not that I don't trust my lawyer, but you are always the best choice.) It's been almost a year now, and you are nearing the end of these little deliveries from me. There will only be a couple more. After all, I couldn't ask the lawyer to continue sending you mail forever, could I? I hope at this point the pain is less, and the fond memories are more. Can you miss someone once you're dead? I don't know the answer to that as I write this, but if it's possible, know that I am missing the two of you. I'm looking down on you, and I will always be here. Lots of love, Cassie

Her handwriting had begun to deteriorate at this point. It was still recognizable, but you could see the effort it took her to pen the words.

I let the tears fall freely. Seeing her write the fact that almost a year had gone by made it more difficult to accept. It seemed like time flew by, leaving me in its dust. The thought that we wouldn't receive any more of her little notes or packages almost broke my heart, although I knew what she said in the note was true. That poor lawyer couldn't be expected to deliver mail forever; he was an attorney not a postman.

I took the little box and the envelope with Brandon's name on it, and put it on the mantle. I would take it with me when we got together tomorrow. The plan was, if the weather cooperated, we would go for a drive, pick up some food and have a picnic somewhere, then get take-out for dinner and come home to eat anniversary cake.

It would give us an opportunity to spend a lot of time together and hopefully have some real conversations. Not that we didn't have real conversations already, but this promised to be an emotionally-charged today.

Aside from this first anniversary, the only day that was going to be more difficult would be the day she actually passed away. That day, I remembered like it was yesterday. It would be seared into my brain for the rest of my life. We sat at her side, Brandon on one side of the bed and me at the other, each of us holding a hand. Her hospice nurse was there too, monitoring the situation.

Cassie had been working tirelessly since she got her diagnosis to ensure she would be able to donate whatever organs were safe and worthy of being donated. After weeks of testing, the doctor and the transplant team had agreed that she was a candidate. Brain tumor patients were very rarely accepted as organ donors, so this was a big deal for her.

Once her hospice nurse had verified that she wouldn't be waking up again, she was transferred to the hospital. Her wish had been to die at home, but once the doctor explained the situation she had agreed to be transferred. As long as her last conscious moments were at home, she said, she was willing to die at the hospital to fulfill the needs of others. That was so like her, giving of herself right up until the very end.

The day of their anniversary dawned clear and bright if a little chilly. Brandon had sent me a text and night before letting me know he would pick me up around eight am. I touched the tiny box and the envelope in my bag, planning to give it to him wherever we decided to have our picnic. I sincerely hoped that the surprise made him happy, rather than making him even more sad. Each of the gifts she had sent to us had that conundrum. We enjoyed receiving things from her, but it reminded us so starkly that she was no longer there to hand them to us in person.

He knocked on the door, letting himself in at precisely eight. "Are you ready to go?" he hollered down the hall.

"I'm coming! I've just been finishing up my hair."

I headed down the hallway, ready to get out the door. I grabbed my jacket and my bag, digging in it to make sure I had my house keys. Twice in the last week, I had left them on the mantle or somewhere, locking myself out.

As we climbed into the truck Brandon wanted to know if I had a specific destination in mind.

"Let's just get on the road, and see where it takes us."

After stopping at a coffee stand and then the taco truck to get breakfast burritos, we were on the highway. We alternated between small talk and stretches of silence that weren't uncomfortable. We wound up in a little town, picking up lunch and driving to their lake shore In spite of the good weather, it was almost empty, thanks to it being the middle of a weekday.

We took our lunch to a little picnic table, looking out at the scenery. As we finished eating I took the little box out of my bag.

"I have something here for you," I said as I handed it over.

"You got me an anniversary gift?" he asked with his eyebrows raised.

"Not exactly," I said, shaking my head.

He looked at me, then down at the familiar

handwriting on the card, and I heard him inhale. He stared at the items for a minute before opening the card. I watched his eyes as he read the note inside. Grief pulled at his features.

He put the card to the side, and slowly untied the ribbon around the box. He removed the lid, setting it gently on the picnic table. With a shaking hand, he removed the contents. It was an ID bracelet, engraved with the date of their wedding and the coordinates of their house, where the wedding had taken place.

"Would you like some help putting it on?" I asked him as he sat and stared at it in silence.

He started to shake his head, then seemed to change his mind. He held out the bracelet and left his wrist extended. It fits in perfectly, of course.

"I love it," I told him softly.

"She always did give the best gifts." He looked up at me and his eyes glistened but no tears fell. "Thank you for doing this, and thank you for being here with me today. I can't tell you how much it means to me."

"No, thank you," I said, "for sharing it with me. I know this is both an extremely special and extremely painful day for you. Anything I can do to be here for you, and I'll do it."

He was quiet for a minute, then met my eyes. "Do you find it a little odd that we are out, pretty much on a date, celebrating the first anniversary of my wedding to my now-dead wife?"

I pondered this question for a minute before answering. "Not really. I see it is a fantastic way of honoring her. I can't imagine a time in my life will come when I don't do things to remember her on every date that was special."

He nodded slowly. "You make a good point."

"Besides, in all honesty, I think this is what she would have wanted. If she could have left instructions for all of us about what to do after she was gone, this probably would have been high on her list. After all, it's not like she hasn't made it known that she's all for it, in spite of not being here to champion it. Of course, if she were actually here the whole situation would be entirely different."

"Isn't it strange how one tiny event in life can cause a ripple effect? I've been pondering the chain of events that led up to her death, and I can't help but wonder if one little thing had been different, would the outcome have changed?"

"Believe it or not, that's exactly what I was thinking the night of your birthday when you were all making fun of me for not paying attention. It's certainly a big concept to try to wrap my head around."

The wind picked up around the Lake, driving us back to the car. Brandon turned on the engine to warm it up, and we sat and chatted for a little while longer. Deciding we wanted to head home for dinner and cake, he backed out of the parking spot and got back on the highway.

As we got back into town and acquired dinner sat quietly in our own thoughts. We pulled up to the house, Cassie's house, and sat in the driveway for a minute. I stared up at it, remembering the day she had brought me to look at it with her. She texted me the day before announcing that she thought she had found "the house."

We drove out and she excitedly showed me all the rooms, the deck off the back, and the pond. She signed papers on it that very same afternoon and lived here until the day she died. Her home had been her happy place. It was still so strange to be in it without her.

Toby was excited to see us both as we let ourselves

in the door. I knelt down on the floor to give him proper attention.

"Hello boy! I'm glad to see you too." I struggled to talk without letting him get his tongue in my mouth as he licked my entire face in his excitement.

Brandon helped me up off the floor as he balanced the take out bags in his other hand. It took until that minute for Toby to realize that in addition to me, *food* also came in the door with us. He immediately turned his attention to Brandon.

"Fickle dog!" I pretended to grumble as I laughed at his complete about face.

As always, we had brought Toby home dinner too, which I put in his dish as Brandon set the table for ours. He took out a bottle of champagne.

"This is from the reception," he said as he held it up.

"Her favorite." I gazed at the label, remembering how she had carefully chosen every last detail of her special day.

As we ate Brandon looked over at me. "I have a proposition for you."

I raised my eyebrows. "Oh really?"

"Not *that kind* of proposition," he laughed.

"Awww." I pretended to be disappointed, drawing a smile from him. I winked, to be sure he knew I teased (sort of).

"I'd like to go to Barcelona for the answer for the anniversary of her death. I know it's short notice, but would you want to go with me? I want to take a small container of her ashes and spread them in the water at the beach where we walked for our honeymoon. Not all of them, just a spoonful or so. I'd have to get a permit to dump the whole thing, and I'm not ready to give them up yet anyways."

"I think that would be fantastic. She'd love it. And I agree about just doing a little. We can put some in one of those tubes that go on the necklace as a memory thing. I can't remember what they're called, but do you know what I'm talking about?"

He nodded as he got up to grab something out of one of the island drawers. "I was hoping you'd say yes." He handed me some papers. "I already booked the hotel and everything since I knew I was going either way, but these are the dates, and the second paper there is the flights I thought I'd book."

I looked them over, taking note that he had booked a different hotel than the one they went to for their honeymoon. That seemed smart to me, so not to make the trip too painful. Not that it would be easy either way.

He had an entire week planned, and the anniversary of her death fell right in the middle of it. If I agreed to the schedule we'd be leaving in ten days. Who was I kidding, "if?" Of course, I would be on that plane with him.

I looked up and met his anxious gaze. "I'm in."

Chapter Twenty-Four

The prospect of hopping on a plane and crossing the Atlantic Ocean both excited me and terrified me at the same time. I'd been to Canada and Mexico so I had a passport, but I'd never left the continent before.

I had ten days to make sure work was all caught up, I had everything I needed packed, and to wrestle with my own guilt about traveling and planning a week-long vacation around the anniversary of my best friend's death. No matter how many times I told myself that this was what she would have wanted, I couldn't stop the nagging little voice in my head.

By the time the day before our flight rolled around, I had everything on my to-do list checked off. My sister Kendall would be stopping by to check on Kate, and I'd done all the shopping I needed to do. My suitcase was packed. The fridge had been cleaned out. Even the laundry was finished.

Brandon had offered to do the driving and would be picking me up at eight the next morning. I set my suitcase next to the front door in preparation until I had to yell at Kate for the fourth time to stop scratching at it. Into the closet it went.

The morning of our departure saw me get out of bed early so that I would be ready when Brandon arrived. He pulled into the drive and I slipped out the door to keep Kate inside. I loaded my suitcase into the back of the truck and we were off. The only stop we made on the way to the airport was to grab a coffee. The warmth of the cup in my hands soothed some of my nerves.

The hustle and bustle of all the people filing through the TSA security lines only added to the anxious feeling of the day. We'd checked our bags and brought only the basics in our carry-ons. As we sat at our gate Brandon pointed out how he had kept Cassie in the dark about where they were going even as they waited to board the plane.

As we settled in our first-class seats he told me about the couple they had met seated across the aisle from them. I laughed at the idea that those around them joined in on the idea of keeping Cassie from learning their destination. My laughter quieted as he explained how she had no idea until they got off the plane because she had slept the entire flight thanks to a headache.

Cassie had relayed the details to me once they returned home, but hearing it from Brandon's perspective gave it a whole new feeling. They each had such different views of many of the same aspects of the trip, both heartrending in their own ways.

The flight itself lasted for hours and I couldn't get a wink of sleep. Even in the comfortable first-class seats my body ached for motion. I limited my liquid intake after my first trip to the minuscule restroom, not wanting to spend any more time in there than absolutely necessary. Even the free wine couldn't tempt me.

We spent the majority of the hours long flight

chatting with each other. As close as we had been through our ties with Cassie, we still had so much to learn about each other on a personal level. I learned his favorite color was green. Not emerald, but more of a hunter. He shook his head when I announced my favorite color to be the same as hers, purple.

"Why does that not surprise me?" he teased.

My shoulders raised in nonchalance. "I don't know, why doesn't it?" My cheeky grin gave away my mirth, in spite of my attempt to be serious.

"For as much as the two of you had in common you are remarkable different."

"Oh yeah? How so?" I couldn't help but be curious as his comparison of us.

He pursed his lips as if trying to decide how best to word his thoughts. "It's hard to pin down the particulars. It's just that sometimes I looked at the two of you together and you could practically be twins, in spite of your physical differences. Like your souls matched even though your bodies didn't."

I burst into tears. "That is the best thing anyone has ever said to me."

"Ah. Don't cry, Jenna. Please?"

"They're good tears, I promise." I sniffled into the tissues the flight attendant had appeared with. "That's just the most perfect description of our friendship that I have ever heard, and I'm so sad she isn't here to hear it with me."

"She knows. I told her once. When we were looking at the photo she printed and framed for you. She said if she had more time she would demand that the two of you got matching tattoos saying as much."

A light bulb went off in my head. "That's exactly what I'll do. I will get the outline of the two of us from that photo and the words underneath. It will be the most perfect memorial tattoo ever."

I could tell the idea had caught him by surprise, but if his growing smile gave any indication, he thought it was a good one. I immediately began planning it in my head, wishing I had a piece of paper in my carry-on bag. I kept a pen in my purse but had nothing to write on. Brandon caught the flight attendant on her way by and made a request.

She returned with a paper bag. "Will this do?"

"It's perfect for now, thank you so much."

I immediately turned my attention to making a

rough sketch of my idea and the phrasing I wanted, so I would be sure to not forget it. My excitement built as I worked on it, thrilled to see the concept come to life right before me as I worked. Art had never been my strong suit, but I got enough to give the artist a good idea when the time came for me to commission it.

The remainder of the flight passed with very little worth writing home about. I peered out the window as we descended over Barcelona. It was night on their side of the globe, so other than the lights of the city I couldn't see much, but the lights were beautiful on their own.

After landing we gathered our luggage and Brandon scheduled an Uber to the hotel. Both of us needed some rest in spite of doing nothing but sitting on the airplane for hours on end. Our arrival at the hotel was met with the news that they had overbooked and they had no doubles left. Only a single queen.

I looked at Brandon and he looked at me. I shrugged.

"I'm so tired I don't care. We can figure it out tomorrow."

He nodded to the clerk and they handed us our keys, promising to move us as soon as the room type we'd reserved opened up. Dumping our suitcases right inside the door, we kicked off our shoes and flopped onto the bed. With only a few hours til morning here, we drifted off into sleep without words.

I opened one eye, squinting at the brightness. We had forgotten to close the curtains before falling into bed the night before, and it just so happened I was the one facing the window. I rolled to my other side and pulled the pillow over my head. Jet lag was a real thing, and I wasn't ready to get up for the day.

My tossing and turning woke Brandon, who turned over to look at me. He smiled.

"Good morning. Are you ready to get up?"

I just groaned. I really wasn't, but I didn't want to spend the majority of our first day sleeping either. He laughed at me and sat up.

"Well, I'm going to take a shower. Do you want me to wake you when I get out?"

I shook my head. "I'm up. I'm up. I'll just get settled while you shower."

He rummaged through his suitcase to get clothes for the day and then disappeared into the bathroom. Our room had a balcony, so I opened the doors and stepped out to look at the surrounding area. Our view showed the town square. There were a couple of small markets, some souvenir shops, and some restaurants.

Barcelona was beautiful. I could see why Cassie had fallen so in love with it. We were close to the beach, so I could smell the salty air but not see it, nor hear the waves. I couldn't wait to get dressed and take a walk down to the ocean. Cassie had told me all about how beautiful it was.

Brandon and I traded places so that I could get ready for the day as well. I dug up some clothes and grabbed my toiletry bag before disappearing into the bathroom. The shower was equipped with a rain head shower head that sounded lovely. The water helped to wash away some of the jet lag.

Making quick work of my morning routine, I exited the bathroom to find Brandon standing on the balcony. He turned towards me as he heard the bathroom door open.

"It's beautiful here, isn't it?" he asked me.

I went over and stood by his side. "Yes, it is. I was just saying to myself while you were in the shower that I can see why Cassie loved it so."

He returned his gaze to the view outside. "She did. She enjoyed every moment we were here."

"I'm looking forward to seeing all of the things she told me about. Her face lit up every time she described something she had seen here."

"Do you want to go get some breakfast?"

My stomach rumbled loudly at just the right moment, causing us both to laugh. "I suppose it's about time to eat if you ask my stomach."

We spent that first day wandering the city. We walked the two blocks down to the beach, Brandon pointing out things that he and Cassie had seen on their trip. We had breakfast at a tiny little hole in the wall restaurant that made the best food.

We gathered brochures for the things we thought we might want to do while we were here. Brandon had planned to show me some of the things that he had already seen, and we wanted to do some new things as well.

We had three full days in Spain before the anniversary and three full days after. Knowing that both of us would be out of sorts and in a somber mood on the anniversary of her death, we planned to do nothing more than walk to the beach to spread her ashes and relax.

We had only brought a tiny container, knowing that in order to actually spread human remains we would have needed a permit. The couple of tablespoons we had chosen to bring were in a small purple box tied with a ribbon, which made it easy to transport as well. We wanted to spread them at either sunrise or sunset, both times of the day the Cassie had loved.

We spent those first three days experiencing the city in much the same way they had on their honeymoon. Many of the things Brandon showed me were places they had been. Each time we visited a new monument or landmark, I pictured Cassie in the setting. It healed my heart some to know that her last trip had been one she wanted to take for her entire life.

There were times I could even match some of the photos she had shown me to the exact location Brandon and I were standing. It was both a healing and sobering experience.

On the eve of the anniversary of her death, Brandon and I were walking back to the hotel as the sun set. He looked over at me.

"Do you think she would approve of us spreading

her ashes here?"

"Absolutely. I think she'd be thrilled to know that a piece of her was in a place that she loved so much."

"I'm struggling with the thought of giving even a piece of her up. I know they're just ashes and she's no longer there, but I feel like it's one of the few things that still tie us together. It's going to be hard for me to let them go."

"You're right, she's no longer with us. But you're wrong in that it's one of the few things you still have to tie the two of you together. You had an entire life together. You have the house and Toby. You have all of your photos and all of your memories. She is still with us, even if we can't see her. And I think she'd be sad that you wanted to hold onto her ashes for that reason."

He frowned, not saying anything for the moment. I reached out and touched his arm.

"We don't have to do it if you don't want to, but I do think it's what she would have wanted."

"No, you're right. This would thrill her to no end. It's just my personal attachments, not that I think she would agree with it. I'm just afraid if I give away too many parts of her, eventually I will have nothing left."

"You'll always have your memories."

"I know, but memories aren't a tangible thing. I can't touch them, or hold them, or look at them. It's almost like they're just barely there, and I'm afraid that eventually even they will fade. I'm terrified of the day I will wake up one morning and possibly have trouble remembering her face or her smell."

I took a minute to formulate my response, not wanting to make his pain worse. There was no easy way to tell him that eventually, those things were going to happen. There would always be photos, but time has a way of fading things that we had no control over.

"I know it's hard now. I struggle in many of the same ways. The only thing that gets me through is reminding myself that she wouldn't want me to feel that way. She's done everything she can in this first year to ensure that we began moving on with our lives. She would be devastated if she knew we were sad over her."

He chuckled. "You're right, she's done everything she can to run things even from wherever she is now."

"Her bossy streak is showing, isn't it? I giggle sometimes thinking just how bossy she is from beyond the grave when she was so laid back when she was here."

"As long as the long list of applicants for a new wife doesn't show up on my doorstep like you mentioned before, I will be okay with it."

Once again the imagery brought on by that situation made me laugh out loud. I could clearly see in my mind's eye a line of women wrapping up the sidewalk onto the front porch, just waiting to hand in their application. Cassie would have vetted at each and every one of them ahead of time, and only sent the best candidates over for an interview.

That evening Brandon took me to what had been Cassie's favorite restaurant on their trip. It was another tiny place, with only six tables and four chairs at each. It had an outside area with a couple more tables, but many people seemed to be coming for takeout. I remembered Cassie telling me about the paella, and that's exactly what I ordered.

When the waitress finally sat it before me, I closed my eyes to picture Cassie sitting here with the exact same plate in front of her. I could see her hands tracing the hand-painted tiles on the tabletop. I said a brief prayer that wherever she was, she was looking down on us and smiling as I ordered her favorite meal.

I open my eyes to see Brandon watching me. "What were you thinking about?"

"I remember her telling me about this restaurant, and what she ordered. Since I was ordering the exact same thing I wanted the picture in my mind's eye of her eating it."

I could see the memory bring a smile to his face. "The only thing she complained about was having to pick the shrimp legs out of her fork. She wanted to be sure she didn't eat any of them at all."

"I can't blame her. They look like they would get stuck in your teeth."

Chapter Twenty-Five

I listened to Brandon toss and turn for most of the night. Since I couldn't be sure if he was just caught up in a restless sleep or actually awake I didn't attempt to talk to him and ask if he wanted to chat. We both knew the coming day would be difficult. After all, that explained why I lay there awake enough to know that his rest sucked too.

By the time dawn began to streak across the sky, Brandon had settled and I had given up on any chance of getting some sleep. I started the tiny coffee maker that sat in our room and went out to the balcony to watch the sun come up.

My emotions were all over the map. Grief swamped me like tsunami waves, sometimes threatening to drown me, and sometimes receding to leave me feeling as if I might make it through the day. I picked up the tiny purple box that held Cassie's ashes, picking at the purple ribbon that held the lid on. I didn't dare open it on the balcony or fear of the wind carrying them away.

As I drank my coffee I heard Brandon begin to toss and turn again. After a moment, I heard him groan followed by a thud.

"Are you alright in there?" I called.

"As all right as I'm ever going to be." I heard him say, voice muffled as though he had buried his head in the covers.

I returned to the room and set the box on the dresser. Brandon turned his head to see what I was doing. He made no move to get up though.

"Do you have any idea how you want to run things today?" I asked him.

Finally, he rolled over and sat up. He looked from me to the little purple box on the dresser, then back at me. He shook his head and shrugged at the same time.

"Well, thanks to my crappy sleep we've already missed sunrise. So we can spend the day doing whatever we'd like, and spread her ashes at sunset?"

"I had pretty crappy sleep too. And I think sunset will be perfect. Is there anything, in particular, you'd like to spend the day doing?"

Another shake of his head. "Nah, let's just go out and see what happens."

"Sounds good to me. I'm going to hop in the shower and get ready for the day. Maybe you can get a little more sleep?"

"Nah, I'm awake now. Time for coffee."

As I finished getting ready for the day, I stepped out of the bathroom to see him standing on the balcony with the tiny purple box cradled in his hands. Not wanting to intrude on his moment I stood there silently, watching him from afar. His shoulders hunched and his head tilted downward as if he were looking at the ground. He made no movement and uttered no sound.

Feeling like I was spying on a personal moment, I turned towards my suitcase to put my dirty clothes in the bag. He must have heard me because as soon as I turned around he stood behind me. He pushed the little box towards my hands.

"I think you're going to have to be the one to dump them. I just don't know if I can bring myself to do it."

I took the box from him and set it on the table. Turning back toward him I grabbed both of his hands in mine. I squeezed them gently.

"We will do it together. And if you decide you can't do it, there's no shame in that. We don't have to dump them at all if that's not what you want to do."

He shook his head before he even began speaking. "No, this is what she would have wanted. I want to spread them here. It's just going to be so hard to let even this tiny bit of her go."

"I think maybe you'll feel a little bit better about it once it's finished."

"I think maybe you're right."

"I was thinking that maybe I would take a picture of you as you spread them in the ocean. Maybe you could walk out to the water so it's up to your knees or so, and I will take it with a silhouette against the sunset. It would make a beautiful memory."

"That's an excellent idea. I will do half, and you can

have the box to do the other half and I will take a picture of you. Maybe we can even find someone to take a picture of the two of us standing in the water with the box."

"I'm sure we can find someone to take a picture of us."

His lips quirked up in a small smile as if the thought made him feel a little bit better about giving up this piece of her. I understood his struggle in a small way, having been fighting some of the same feelings within myself. I wanted to keep every single thing that reminded me of her. The only thing pushing me on was knowing how thrilled Cassie would be to know that we had traveled all this way to unite a small part of her with the city that she had loved.

We finished getting ready for the day and headed out into town. I think both of us unconsciously did our best to keep busy so we didn't dwell on what was going to happen later that afternoon. We took a hop-on-hop-off bus tour, one that went outside of town and showed us some of the surrounding countryside.

We had lunch, visited a museum, and walked through some small souvenir shops. The weather was perfect, sunny and neither too hot or too cold. Before we knew it was time to head back to the hotel room. We had about an hour left until Sunset, and I wanted to change before we went to the beach.

Brandon had given me the sun hat Cassie had worn for their honeymoon, and I had chosen to wear it today. It was one more way to honor her memory. Because I had intended to take Brandon's picture spreading the ashes all along, I had brought a five by seven photograph of Cassie for him to hold. It was one he had taken of her on the very beach we planned to release her ashes.

She had one arm up in the air and one on her hat, keeping the breeze from blowing it away. Her long hair floated about her, and the smile on her face was just barely visible thanks to the setting sun behind her. It truly captured Cassie's essence, her positivity and joy radiated even from the printed paper.

I tucked it carefully into my purse with the little purple box. I checked my phone's battery to be sure we wouldn't have trouble taking the photos. Deciding I was ready to go, I took a seat in the armchair facing the balcony and waited for Brandon to finish.

We walked down to the beach arm in arm, neither of us having much to say. We arrived at the boardwalk with about 15 minutes to spare before sunset. We both kicked off our shoes and headed down to the water's edge. Along the way, I bent over to pick up tiny pieces of sea glass mixed in with the sand. I wanted to save some as a memento. I hoped to find a cute glass jar to hold sand and sea s\glass, perhaps mixing it with a tiny bit of her ashes to keep at home.

As the sun sank lower on the horizon I looked at Brandon. "Are you ready?" I asked him gently.

He started to shake his head, then nodded. "I don't know that I can get any more ready. I think it's going to hurt no matter how ready I think I am."

I took the tiny purple box and the photograph out of my purse, handing them to him. Grabbing my phone, I instructed him where I wanted him to stand. In my attempt to get the right angle, with the right lighting, I probably took twenty shots. I knew at least one of them would turn out to be a good one.

We traded places and he took some of me holding the box and the picture. We were then lucky enough to find a kind couple walking the beach to take some of both of us. Thanking them, I took my phone back and scrolled through the shots we had captured. We had plenty and it was time.

"I've got all the photos we need. Whenever you're ready Go ahead."

He looked at me in silence, then turned his attention down to the little box in his hands. The grief on his face was plain to see, and I knew he was struggling. I also knew that this was something he needed to get through on his own, I didn't want to intrude.

He slowly untied the ribbon with shaking hands. My heart broke as I watched the tears leak out of his eyes and roll down his cheeks. Even with the ocean waves, I imagined I could see the teardrops hitting the surface of the salty water, his grief mingling with the ocean, where some of Cassie's ashes would forever stay.

A slight breeze swept across the beach. The sky turned brilliant tones of purple and orange. A hush seemed to fall over the area, and I could hear nothing other than the waves crashing against the sand. It was almost as if the ocean was asking Brandon to share her with it.

As he lifted the lid off the box, he turned to look

back at me. I wiped my tears and gave him a smile, nodding to encourage him. Instead of dumping the box, he put the lid back on and waved for me to join him.

I waded out to meet him, the waves catching the hem of my dress and soaking it.

"I need your help." His voice was husky with his grief.

I nodded and reached for his hand, lacing my fingers through his and giving it a squeeze. I held the picture in my other hand, and he held the box on his opposite side. For just a moment I close my eyes and let the breeze caress me in silence.

I kept them closed as I heard Brandon's choked voice beside me. "Cassie, I loved you so damn much. There will never be a day that I don't miss you, and I know this isn't really goodbye. None of this has been. I know how much you loved this beach, so I've brought a piece of you to always stay here. I know this isn't you anymore, but I have such a hard time giving even a little bit of you up."

My tears fell unchecked down my cheeks and I squeezed Brandon's hand a little tighter. For a moment the grief threatened to suffocate me, worse than any drowning waves could ever feel. Opening my eyes, I looked over to see him watching me. His hand returned the pressure of my squeeze and I felt a connection between us that has never been there before. Something different blooming from this moment in time.

We were sharing a moment that neither of us would forget for a very long time. I smiled at him the best I could, hoping to encourage him. His head bowed and he took one last look at the ashes in the little purple box. With a weeping wind to help them along, he turned the box upside down.

"Fly free Cassie. I love you."

We stood in the ocean waves together for some time afterward. Our hands remained intertwined, neither of us feeling the need to speak. Before we headed back towards shore, he pulled me close and wrapped his arms around me, holding me tightly. I returned the gesture, leaning my cheek against his chest.

I felt his lips brush the top of my head. In response I gently dug my fingertips into the muscles of his back, acknowledging his gesture.

"Thank you," he whispered. "I don't know if I could have done this without you."

"Thank you for bringing me. I'm so honored you chose to include me."

Hand in hand we returned to the spot on the beach where we had left our shoes. Collecting them we continued up to the boardwalk and back towards the room. The mood was somber, but also content.

As we reached the hotel room both of us seemed overcome by awkwardness. A new awareness had somehow been opened by the sharing of that emotional act, and neither of us knew what to do with it. Finally, Brandon looked at me, meeting my eyes.

"Is it just me?"

In spite of the vague phrasing of his question, I knew exactly what he asked. I shook my head. "No."

"I don't know what to do."

"Me either."

If anyone had told me one year ago I would be standing in a hotel room, in Spain, with my best friend's widower, fighting the urge to make our relationship more than a friendship, I would have laughed at them. I would have been offended, even. Yet here I stood, in that very situation. The even crazier part of the equation was that it wasn't just one-sided. I could see him struggling too.

"Do you feel the guilt?" His brow creased as he forced the question past his lips.

I nodded, unable to voice the answer. At times the guilt suffocated me.

"She'd want us to be happy."

"If we are to believe the notes she wrote us, yes."

"I just... I don't..." he shrugged, letting the sentence trail off without completing it.

Deciding to table the conversation or another time, I got control of my voice and smiled. "What do you say we just worry about dinner for now?"

Part of him seemed to want to carry on the conversation, but I could see the relief in his eyes as well. We both needed to come to terms with how we felt.

"Sounds good."

He slipped his arm around my shoulders and we headed out the door. There would be plenty of time to talk later.

Chapter Twenty-Six

Clouds had moved in and blanketed the sky while we were in the hotel room. I worried about our lack of umbrella since we chose to walk to dinner. Brandon pointed out we could always take an Uber home and we continued to the restaurant.

Dinner devolved into tasting different sangrias followed up by dessert and more drinks. For a while, I wondered if Brandon was making an attempt to drown his sorrows, but he seemed to be doing okay. He laughed at me as I stumbled out the restaurant door, unsteady on my feet in spite of consuming less than half the drinks he had.

I grabbed his arm. "Do not make fun me, you lush. I had half the drinks you did." I very carefully enunciated my words, ensuring he could understand me.

He laughed even harder. "I'm not making fun of you. You're cute."

"Cute?" I sputtered, unsure of how to answer him.

He hooked his arm through mine, steadying me for the walk back. Luckily we hadn't gone too far, and I had chosen to wear flat, comfortable shoes instead of something fashionable. The more I walked the more I struggled as the alcohol made its way into my system. I didn't even make it back to the room before needing to stop and use the restroom, Brandon chuckling some more as he leaned against the wall outside to wait for me.

As I washed my hands I took a good look at myself in the mirror. How did I get so tipsy? That sangria must have been something else. I sighed, and made my way back to Brandon, shaking my head at myself.

"What's wrong, Jen?"

"What was in those drinks? I may not be a serious

drinker, but usually, I can hold my alcohol better than this."

"Maybe it's just because it's unfamiliar to your system?" He didn't seem too concerned about it.

We made it back to the hotel room without incident, aside from me dancing outside the door while he dug out the key, praying I would make it into the bathroom before I wet myself.

"I'm going to take a shower!" I called through the door, not even bothering to wait and see if he heard me. He'd hear the water running and figure it out.

I took my time, hoping to wash away some of the effects of the drinks. Stepping out of the shower I dried off and paused. I hadn't grabbed myself any clothes. No pajamas, not even a robe. I didn't really feel like putting my dress back on. I huffed, irritated that the towel didn't provide enough coverage.

"Hey Brandon?" I opened the door a tiny crack.

"Yeah? Are you alright in there?"

"Well, yeah. But could you grab me the pajamas off the top of my suitcase? Or my robe? Anything? I didn't plan ahead very well this time."

Seconds of silence ticked by. "What if I say no?"

"Then you're likely to get a view of my pale, white ass because this towel does not even begin to cover everything it should."

He laughed and I heard him get up. A moment later he stood outside the bathroom door. "Here."

I opened the door a little wider and stuck my arm out, waving it around a little. I expected him to hand it over, but I couldn't feel a thing. I peeked through the crack to see him standing just out of reach, my robe dangling from his hand.

"What are you doing? Give me that!"

He extended his arm, still leaving me about a foot shy of being able to get my hands on it. "Come and get it."

"You're asking for trouble big guy." I lurched forward, thinking I'd be able to catch him by surprise and snatch it from him. No such luck. Either he had fantastic reflexes or the sangria had left me at below optimal operation. Either way, I still needed to get covered.

"Shouldn't drink so much, eh?" he teased me from just beyond my range.

I raised an eyebrow. "Like you're one to talk?"

"Well, I am almost a foot taller than you and probably outweigh you by a hundred pounds. My capacity is way better than yours."

"You know what? Forget it."

Adjusting the towel to cover as much as possible, I flung the bathroom door open and stalked past him to my suitcase. I dug through it one-handed, attempting to keep myself covered as I selected something to wear to bed. Brandon hadn't uttered a sound since I'd come from behind the bathroom door.

Turning around with pajamas in hand I found him unabashedly staring at me, lips parted.

"Can I help you? Not that you deserve it since you couldn't be bothered to help me."

He looked like a fish as he opened and closed his mouth, perhaps attempting to make words but failing. He shook his head and silently lifted his arm, holding out the offending robe.

"Well, I don't need it now, silly. I have my clothes." Stepping back into the bathroom I shut the door in his face with a solid thunk, grinning to myself as I did so.

I busied myself with the task of getting ready for bed, unconcerned with whether he had recovered or not.

The situation left me feeling pleased with my course of action. Served him right. I hadn't thought about it beforehand, but considering that he'd been celibate for about a year now, I hoped he was paying for the little trick he thought he would play.

"Your turn," I announced, as I opened the door and went over to put my things back in my suitcase.

He sat in the only armchair in the room, his eyes roaming over my now-dressed form. Other than blinking more rapidly than normal there were no outward signs of distress, although I could read him well enough to know that I had left him shaken.

"Jenna..." His voice was hoarse. His fingers dug into the arms of the chair as if the words required more effort than he had to give.

"Yes?" My voice came out breathy, even though I hadn't intended it to. The tension in the room had shot sky high and I could barely keep from trembling.

"Come here."

I set the stuff in my hands down on top of my suitcase and turned to face him. He stood but didn't make an attempt to close the distance between us. Desire rolled through me, followed by a wave of uncertainty bordering on guilt. In the space of a few seconds, dozens of thoughts ran through my head.

How had I come to feel this way about Brandon, when I would never have even thought of him in this manner before Cassie died?

Would she really be okay with the two of us getting together?

Those weren't the only two but they carried the theme for my internal monologue. I took two steps in his direction, then waited for him to meet me halfway. Maybe a little more than halfway, but he started it. He took a single step forward, leaving just within arm's reach of each other. I shivered.

"Are you cold?"

"No," I whispered, shaking my head as I rubbed my hands over my arms.

"Hm. I could warm you up?"

"I find it more than likely you would set me on fire..." I let the sentence trail off as I met his deep blue eyes. "And I don't want to get burned."

"Are you scared?"

I said the word no while nodding my head yes, extending my hands out, palms up in confusion. He took the last step to bring us inches apart while laying his palms on top of mine. The warmth of his touch chased away the shivers, for the moment.

I looked up at him. "Are you ready for this?"

"To be honest, I'm not sure what all I'm ready for but I know that the feelings I've developed for you aren't wrong, and they're not going away." His breath shuddered when he exhaled, causing mine to do the same as I inhaled.

As his arm snaked around my waist I ran my hands up his biceps, curling one around the back of his neck and the other trailing down across his chest. His free hand came up to cup my chin, tilting my head back.

As our lips met the clouds that had made their appearance earlier in the evening let loose with a rumbling thunder. The rain poured down from the sky, bouncing off the balcony tile and in through the open doors. We paid it no mind, drinking each other in as if we were the only port in the storm.

Brandon took two steps backward toward the bed, dragging me with him and never releasing my lips. I felt the jolt as he reached the edge of the mattress, sitting down hard and bringing me onto on his lap. Our hands explored the peaks and valleys of each other's bodies, touching in a way we had never come together before.

As the urgency receded we found ourselves stretched out side by side. I lay curled in his embrace, enjoying the process of getting to know each other on a more intimate level. Brandon raised his head and smiled at me. I returned an answering grin.

"I think we let the carpet get wet."

He laughed. "It will dry."

"That was quite the storm." I ran my hand over his bicep as I spoke.

He raised an eyebrow at my double meaning. "Why yes, yes it was."

He rolled off the bed, extending his hand to help me up and led me to the balcony. The storm had passed as quickly as it rolled in, leaving blue skies peeking through the rain clouds. We looked toward the beach, and I gasped.

A beautiful double rainbow stretched from one side of the city to the other. It immediately made me think of Cassie.

"I think she approves," I murmured.

Brandon nodded in agreement, kissing my temple.

"I think she does."

THE END

ABOUT THE AUTHOR

Tera Lyn Cortez lives in the Pacific Northwest with her husband and five children, plus an assortment of pets. When she's not writing she is a voracious reader and loves to travel.

She is also a lover of all things chocolate and can be found communing with the ocean whenever possible.

Visit her website or Facebook page to make a connection!

https://www.teralyncortez.com/

http://www.facebook.com/teralyncortez

Sign up for her newsletter here!

https://sendfox.com/teralyncortez

OTHER BOOKS
by Tera Lyn Cortez:

Just Once More

The Soul Scribe Trilogy:

ISOLATION

INVOCATION

INAUGURATION

The Soul Scribe Omnibus, Books 1-3

MIDNIGHT WHISPERS ANTHOLOGY
Coming March 2021